Scandal at Christmas

THE NOBLE LORDS: BOOK 4

DANELLE HARMON

OLIVERHEBERBOOKS

COPYRIGHT 2015 © Danelle Harmon

Published by Oliver-Heber Books & Gnarly Wool Publishing

0 9 8 7 6 5 4 3 2 1

MORE IN THIS SERIES

THE NOBLE LORDS

Master of My Dreams

Taken by Storm

Scandal at Christmas

My Saving Grace

PROLOGUE

WINTER 1813, LONDON

Agatha Pemberly, the Countess of Weston, sighed.

Had it been any other debutante, dowager, or respected matron, well then, that soft exhalation of air might have been perceived as rather insignificant.

Except Agatha gathered after a more than twenty-year friendship with Lady Clare Carlisle, Lady Pamela Portland, and Lady Lenore Penmore, her dear friends should by now know the following:

One sigh signified news of importance.

Two sighs indicated a matter of concern.

And three sighs, well, three sighs bordered on call-the-constable-there-is-trouble-indeed. Agatha, the leader of their little group since they'd met at Mrs. Thistelwait's Finishing School twenty-four years ago, now passed her gaze over the trio she'd assembled. She studied them as they chatted. With their unfettered laughs and wildly gesticulating hands, they may as well have been just ladies meeting for tea. She furrowed her brow. Except they were something far more than that.

They were four *mamas* meeting for tea.

She gave her head a deploring shake. These were sad days indeed if her friends, all parents to a collection of unwed daughters, could be so...so...immune to the great peril their offspring faced.

With a frown, Agatha sighed.

Again.

She tipped the porcelain teapot over and filled three empty cups to the brim with the steaming brew. And waited.

Clare picked up her cup of tea and blew on the contents. The stiffly proper mama made to take a small sip, then froze. "Oh, dear." She blinked several times. "Was that three sighs?"

"Four," Agatha corrected. Humph. They'd *not* been attending as they should. "There were four." She winged a brow up. "Four sighs."

With her cup halfway to her lips, Lenore stilled. "Oh, my." The delicate porcelain cup in her fingers trembled slightly and she quickly set it down.

Having at last secured the other matrons' attention, Agatha took one more sip of her tea and put the half-empty contents down beside Lenore's now forgotten refreshment. Each woman edged forward in their seats and then looked expectantly at her. *Well, at last.*

Appreciating that her friends now attended her, Agatha smoothed her palms over her silvery satin skirts and took a deep breath. "It is—" She paused and glanced around the room. She peered across the room at the floor-length windows. With her gaze, she searched for slippered feet. After all, a mother could never be too careful with a precocious, and often troublesome, young daughter underfoot. Content that her search revealed no hidden minxes, she spoke in a loud whisper, "It is Jane."

The trio of ladies tipped their heads in a like manner.

Surely they followed the reason for this visit now? Except Pamela wrinkled her brow. She looked back and forth between the other two ladies. The lady's perplexed expression matched the one she'd worn as a girl of fifteen struggling through her French lessons.

Agatha turned a pointed stare on Clare. They shared a look. Then, the ever proper marchioness patted Pamela's knee. "The Season. She is speaking of Jane's dism— er"—the other woman had the good grace to flush—"Season."

Pamela widened her eyes. "Ahh." She smiled widely, also with the same pleased grin as when she'd *mastered* parts of those long ago French lessons. But then her smile dipped. "Oh."

At last. Agatha moved closer to the edge of her seat. "My Jane had a dismal first Season." The other women were too polite to agree, but too honest to not issue false protest. "Her second Season." She shook her head and winced. "Well, her second Season was a good deal worse."

Her supportive friends nodded commiseratively.

"Nowhere near as dire as my Winnie's," Pamela muttered from under her breath. She wrinkled her nose. "I have it on good authority from her brother, Thomas —" She tapped her fingertip against her lip. "Or perhaps it was James, which makes a good deal more sense because Thomas is away at univ—"

A sound of impatience escaped Clare. "Pamela," she scolded. Through their years of friendship, Lady Carlisle had proven the most coolly logical of the friends. "I believe we are attending Agatha's concerns."

My concerns?

Agatha eyed the other woman disapprovingly. How for all her logic and reason could Clare not have the sense the Lord gave a horse to demonstrate a suitable degree of alarm for her own unwed daughter as well? She sighed. Then, Clare had always demonstrated a remarkable faith in her children. *Tsk, tsk.* Silly woman.

"She has gone all quiet," Lenore whispered loudly.

Three pairs of eyes snapped to Agatha once more.

She patted her meticulous coif. After all, they'd all learned well by now that silence oft preceded one of her telling and very deliberate sighs. "We were speaking of our daughters." Agatha took a moment to level them each with a look. "Our *unwed* daughters."

"I daresay we do not require the whole unwed business attached to it, Agatha," Lenore said with a dry note underscoring her words. "We all know precisely the marital state of our daughters."

Agatha pounced. "Do we, though?" She sent another eyebrow shooting up. "Do we, when we should speak so casually of the cherry tarts made by Cook—"

Their plump friend shifted on her seat. "They *were* delicious tarts," Pamela mumbled underneath her breath.

As one, the group gave her yet another look.

"Er, right," Pamela said with a shake of her head. "Well then, as I was saying, my Winnie," she dropped her voice to a scandalized whisper, "has set her sights upon a particular gentleman," A frown turned her lips. "A gentleman whose identity I still haven't gleaned." She took a sip of her tea and then set it down hard enough to send liquid droplets spraying over the table. "But I will. I assure you I will find out."

"I consider myself fortunate to have just my Jane to wed off." With but one daughter, Agatha would inspire envy in any mama trying to make a match with a daughter who'd never be considered a diamond of the first waters.

"Do you know my Winnie insists she'll not wed because her heart is otherwise engaged?" As though pained by the very idea of it, a groan escaped the plump Pamela. She plucked a pastry from the tray of treats upon the rose-inlaid table and took a large bite.

The group fell silent. Who could have ever anticipated when they'd been young girls of fifteen in finishing school that such woes awaited them as beleaguered mamas? Only with a mother's insight did they now know that those distinguished institutions should add the very important course of marrying-ones-daughter-off to the lessons on deportment and embroidery.

Pamela made to reach for another confectionary creation when Agatha drummed her fingertips upon the arms of her chair. "Were we ever so...so...*hopelessly romantic?*"

An inelegant snort escaped Lenore. "Indeed, we were not. We were practical..."

"Logical," Clare supplied. She gave a wry smile.

"And determined to make a good match," Agatha added that last, very important point. Which brought her neatly back to the very reason she'd summoned her dear friends over on this ungodly chilly, snowy, winter day. Pamela leaned over and picked up another tart from the quickly dwindling tray.

Agatha drew in a deep breath finding the strength to utter words that had no place being spoken aloud. But then, theirs was a very special friendship, only strengthened over time. There were no secrets among them. "I fear if I...er, that is *we*, do not intervene then my Jane will be in a very dire situation. *Very dire*," she said with just enough dramatic flourish to call Pamela's attention away from the pastries. "Your Winifred is in equal amounts of trouble."

The woman's plump fingers fluttered back to her side.

Agatha glanced around the small pairing of friends she'd assembled. "As is your Prudence." Clare's eyes formed moons. She continued on to Lenore. "And as is your Leticia."

"But what can we do?" Lenore tossed her hands up. "I cannot get my girl to think of anything other than ...her horses."

The other three mamas fell immediately silent, as though fearing one of their lamentable children might be very well lurking outside the closed parlor door.

Agatha cleared her throat and took care to speak in low, hushed tones. "Why, there is only one thing we can do. As concerned mothers, that is."

Her three friends looked back at her and then Agatha gave a slow, conspiratorial smile.

Lenore's brow went up in a dawning realization. She scrambled forward to the edge of the pale pink upholstered sofa. "Dare we?" she asked breathless. "They'll never forgive us if they discover what we've done."

Agatha scoffed. "I imagine it far more likely they'll never forgive us if they grow into lonely, unwed spinsters."

"*What* are we doing?" Pamela stomped her slippered foot, a rather awkward feat considering her position perched at the edge of her seat.

Clare took heart. "Do pay attention. They are interfering, my dear." She pointed her eyes to the ceiling.

Agatha pursed her lips. Did Clare believe herself above matchmaking? Oh, poor, poor Clare. Ever the voice of reason, and in this case, deplorable reason, she turned her lips up in one of those I-know-so-much-more-than-you smiles. "I do believe some of us," she gave Agatha a look, "are given to histrionics."

Not rising to the other woman's bait, Agatha picked up her teacup and took a sip.

"I've little worries where my Prudence is concerned," Clare said with a flounce of her hair. "She is practical and reasonable and logical." *Like me.* The marchioness leaned forward and poured herself another cup of tea.

Lenore and Agatha exchanged another look from over her head. Poor, hopelessly blind Clare. Well, it was their duty to help her *and* her daughter, whether the other ladies themselves failed to see as much.

"Whatever shall we do?" Pamela moaned, bringing them back to the crucial matter that brought them here this day. Even the flighty one of their group saw the peril.

Agatha waited a moment until each pair of eyes was fixed solely on her. Then, with a very precise movement, she turned her lips up in a slow, mischievous smile. "We will be playing *matchmakers* this Christmas."

Silence met her pronouncement.

Pamela wrung her hands together. "Oh, but will they *ever* agree to any match we dare suggest?" And much the way she'd done as a nervous debutante, she reached for yet another pastry and began to nibble away at Cook's latest creation.

Agatha moved her finger in a deliberate circle. "Ahh, but we wouldn't dare do anything as direct as to suggest the gentlemen best suited for our wayward girls."

A smile to rival the cat who'd found Cooks' cream split Lenore's cheeks. "Why, I daresay if we even discourage their attention, we might be best served."

At that, Pamela paused mid-bite. She reached for a napkin and dabbed at her lips. "Whyever would we discourage them from..." Then her eyes lit. "I see."

At last. As had been Pamela's way through the years, inevitably she caught on.

Their dear, if obstinate, daughters would never do something as agreeable as making the match their mothers knew to be for the best. If, however, they gave them necessary guidance through some very deliberate *misguidance*, well then, Agatha rather suspected every single one of their incorrigible, four eldest, unwed daughters would find themselves wed—by the Christmas holiday if Agatha, Pamela, Lenore, and Clare had their way.

And invariably, the four resolute mamas always had their way.

Always.

DECEMBER 1813, NORFOLK, ENGLAND

S he was good at eavesdropping.

To the servants who were dusting the paintings that hung in the portrait gallery of this grand house that she and her mother were visiting, the Honourable Miss Letitia Ponsonby, only daughter of Lord and Lady Penmore, was a study in perfection. Perfect posture as she sat in a chair reading just outside a drawing room door. Perfect hair, a lustrous blend of amber and gold, parted, pinned and encircled in a teal velvet band from which tiny curls escaped to frame her heart-shaped face. Perfect silence as she engrossed herself in the small book open in her lap.

Silence was, of course, necessary for perfect eaves-dropping.

She sat primly at the edge of her chair, her pelisse of pale blue-green velvet arranged carefully around her. Her slippers, white lace over a color that mirrored the sea on which her father had made his fame and fortune, peeped out from beneath the hem of her muslin gown, each toe set against the line that separated one marble tile from another. A true lady was the beautiful Letitia but only her mother, quietly conversing behind that closed door with their host, Lady Ariadne, knew that appearances were deceiving...and how acute her daughter's hearing actually was.

Letitia could hear the words as clearly as if she had pressed her ear to the ancient wood panel.

"It is good to see you again after so long, Ariadne. I hope you know how grateful my Lettie and I are for the invitation to stay here with you on our way down to Leeds, especially with the roads being as they are this time of year. Frankly, I'd have never left Lincolnshire to make such a long trip, but when Lady Weston summons one to her home, one must go. The situation has become critical, I'm afraid."

"Situation?"

"Our daughters. And especially *my* daughter, Letitia. Wild as the wind she is, and still unmarried. Seth and I despair of her ever making a match. What man would wed a young lady who walks the fence line between respectability and scandal? My Lettie cares for nothing but horses and the freedom to do as she pleases, and it's probably my fault, as I have never taken a firm hand with her. The mold has been cast, and it is too late to change it."

Letitia sat very still, willing even her heartbeat to pause for a moment. She hid a smile. This was getting interesting.

"My friends are all in the same boat, and if we pull any more hair out over the unmarried state of our daughters, we'll all be as bald as a newly-laid egg. It's why Lady Weston summoned us down to Kent and why we're making this trip. She, the Countess of Portland, and the Marchioness of Carlisle are all despairing over this ... this *situation* every bit as much as I am. It's gone from being embarrassing to downright alarming, I tell you. Four of the loveliest girls in England from four of the oldest and most prestigious families and they are still quite happily unmarried."

"So what will you do?"

"Do? What can I do?" Letitia heard the plaintive wail in her mother's voice and could just picture her wringing her hands. "The only thing I *can* do. Desperate times call for desperate measures, and I am beyond desperate. I have sent word to the Honourable Mr. Homer Trout, inviting him to this same Christmastide house party that we're attending. The Captain and I have already made it quite clear that we would encourage his pursuit of our daughter's hand."

In her chair, Letitia actually *did* feel her heartbeat stop.

Homer *Trout?*

Encourage the pursuit of our daughter's hand?

Her head jerked up and she stared blankly at the opposite wall, her throat tightening, the blood draining from her face. Shock rendered her temporarily unable to think beyond a single silent, plaintive cry: *Mama! Mama, how could you* do *this to me?*

"It is my opinion," her mother was saying, "that the Honourable Mr. Trout will suit my Lettie well. He is mannerly, staid, solid as a rock and quite capable, I suspect, of reining in a girl of her wild and ungovernable nature. In short, quite suitable even if he is not, shall I say, a man to exactly turn a young lady's head."

Homer *Trout?* The blood rushed back to Letitia's face. Panic rose within her as her mother continued blithely on:

"In any case, the deed is done and Homer will be ready and waiting at this house party and this problem will finally be solved," she said with chipper finality. "But enough of me. How are things with you? I understand Colin recently had a paper on colic accepted by the Royal Veterinary College. Such an intelligent man you married, Ariadne. And how are the horses? The farm? Rumor has it you're in need of a head groom."

"Oh, not me, but my brother Tristan. His ran off after Amir bit him one too many times, nearly taking a finger. The man had had enough. It's a shame, really. Amir is a gorgeous colt, so much like his sire and his full brother but oh, he's got teeth and he knows how to use them."

"Is this one of the Norfolk Thoroughbreds that your father, the late earl, spent forty years developing?"

"Yes, and this colt is particularly stunning...I would have kept him here with us, but now that he's got his life in order following all that nasty business from a few years back, Tristan wanted to raise him up at the family pile just west of here in Burnham Thorpe. It would be nice, though, if he could find someone willing to work with the little devil. You don't know of anyone, do you?"

Letitia froze, a crazy, half-baked idea taking shape in her suddenly desperate mind.

"Sadly, I do not," her mother was saying, and Letitia heard the clink of a china cup against a saucer. "But even though my family is one of mariners, we're connoisseurs of fine bloodstock ourselves. I understand the need for reliable help, especially to oversee the development and care of something as priceless as one of your Norfolk Thoroughbreds."

Letitia stood up.

She had two choices. On the one hand was Homer Trout, pale and insipid and with a conical brown mole on the side of his nose from which a hair the length of an eyelash sprouted, a hair that was as stiff and short as a bristle and which would make the act of kissing him an exercise in the personal grooming of her own skin. On the other hand was a Norfolk Thoroughbred colt who dined on people's fingers.

If there was one thing Letitia knew her mother to be, it was determined.

Clever.

And as unswerving in her course as Nelson at Trafalgar.

She had to buy time. To do something, anything, to gain opportunity to decide how to address this newest and most shocking development. She needed to think, and Letitia Ponsonby did so best on the back of a horse.

I have to see this colt. I can slip out for an hour or so and Mama, who takes a nap in the afternoon, will never miss me.

If nothing else, a stiff bracing gallop and time spent admiring some of the finest horseflesh in the world would give her time to figure out how to address the matter of Homer Trout. To even beg off going to this house party, if it came down to it.

Resentment filled her. It wasn't often that she got to visit with her childhood friends Jane, Winnie and Pru, but the knowledge that Homer Trout would be there changed everything. Now, it seemed like a trap where he waited, complete with mole and bristle. Now it seemed like the end of her freedom. She had to think fast if she wanted to out-think, outsmart, and outmaneuver her mother.

There was no time to lose.

She hurried back to her rooms and there found her maid, Beryl, laying out her clothes for the evening meal.

"Beryl, I am going riding in order to clear my head before dinner. Please lay out the breeches I wear under my riding habit, and find me a plain shirt and a boy's waistcoat. A coat, too, as it is cold."

"M' lady?" the maid asked, eyes widening.

Letitia smiled and laid a reassuring hand on the maid's shoulders. "I intend to sneak out for only an hour or two, but I have to do it in disguise. I have no chaperone as you don't ride, and Mama would never approve of my going out riding alone. It will cause talk. So find me the clothes of a boy."

"Beggin' y'r pardon, m' lady, but Oi think that's flirtin' with danger."

"It is only dangerous if I get caught. I don't intend to get caught, only to go look at a horse at a nearby farm and come right back. No one will be the wiser. It is all perfectly safe, I can assure you."

"Ooh, Oi don't loike the sound of this, Oi don't."

"As far as anyone else is concerned, you know nothing about it. Now be a dear, Beryl, and do find me some appropriate clothes."

2

G od and the devil below, he hated Christmas.
Hated the damp winter days, one after another lasting from November all the way into late March, maybe even April, each one full of mist and dull gray clouds that hung so low to earth that one forgot that blue sky existed somewhere above. Raw, bone-chilling cold off the North Sea and rising damp in an ancestral home with which he was struggling to keep up the repairs. Winter, of course, with its drearily short days and expectations of being "happy" in the Christmas season, was not, and never would be, his favorite time of year. The cold and damp aside, the reality that all work stopped so that everyone could celebrate the season and be idle when he had no *time* to be idle, only served to remind him with relentless persistence that it wasn't just a season of cold.

It was a season of loneliness and regret.

He was still unmarried. He had given his beautiful sister Ariadne away to her naval captain-turned-veterinarian two years past, and they were enjoying their growing family and the sight of Norfolk Thoroughbreds cavorting through pastures of thick winter mud. They knew cozy fires and the laughter of children and the pleasure of their own company on a cold winter night, and Tristan St. Aubyn, the Earl of Weybourne, was happy for them.

"Why don't you join us for Christmas this year, Tristan?" Ari had asked, riding over to visit him a fortnight past.

He had pretended to consider, though the joy and happiness of his sister's family only served to highlight all that he had done wrong, all that he was missing, in his own life. Someone to warm his bed at night, someone with whom to enjoy his life's passions, someone to laugh with, cry with, dream with, love with. But he had not found anyone who shared his passions, whose eyes lit up when he talked horses and the continuation of his father's legacy—the Norfolk Thoroughbred, the fastest horses in the world. Most of the herd that his father had spent a lifetime developing had been lost with the exception of a single stallion, Shareb-er-rehh, and the beautiful mare Gazella. Tristan had made it his own life's work to pick up where his father had left off. That left no time for London Seasons or courting. Besides, most women he'd ever met didn't want to talk about horses; they wanted to gossip, discuss fashion, and pretend to be simpering, swooning, delicate little flowers. Perhaps some were but most, Tristan had long since decided, were not delicate flowers at all, but thorn bushes; tougher than they looked, ruthless, and all too willing to cause harm.

He didn't have time to seek a wife, anyhow.

And even if he did, he didn't have time to devote to her, didn't have time to get off this relentless, ever-churning wheel that was business ventures and stocks and evaluating bloodstock and working, working, working, to restore all that he, in the recklessness of his youth, had squandered.

Not even for Christmas.

His father, kind but distant, and putting his horses before his own two children for as long as Tristan could remember, had died three years past, but not before he'd learned of the terrible trouble that his only son and heir had managed to get himself into. Eager for a father figure and full of the enthusiasm and invincibility of youth, Tristan had fallen under the influence of an unscrupulous villain who had stolen from him, blackmailed him, and threatened the lives of those he loved. The whole affair had left him deeply ashamed of his terrible judgment, and all but destitute. In the years since, he had worked long and hard to rebuild his fortunes—and a reputation and legacy of his own of which his father would be proud.

Work, work, work. Really, he had no time to even be

thinking about Christmas and what other people were doing. What he might be doing if he didn't have so much to atone for, if even to himself.

The surviving Norfolk Thoroughbreds were his inheritance, not just his work, though in many senses they were both. The stallion Shareb-er-rehh was Ariadne's horse through and through, though it was to Tristan that he'd been bequeathed and rightfully belonged. But Shareb's yearling son was here now, and he looked to be as nice if not better in conformation, drive, and sheer talent than his legendary sire.

Unfortunately, he had not inherited Shareb's kind disposition.

Tristan drummed his fingers against the table, thinking. Too bad Amir's last groom had become fed up with the colt's surly, dangerous temperament and left. Now he had to put out a search for a new one.

Oh, there were plenty of grooms to be had, but for the princely, temperamental heir of Shareb-er-rehh? It would have to be someone special. Brave. Gifted, even. Tristan considered elevating one of the junior grooms, but the colt was a nasty piece of work and he didn't want to subject anyone else's fingers—or other unwary body parts—to his unpredictable temper.

Besides, not a groom in the stable would go near the colt.

And now this letter that had just come to him from Leeds in Kent and his old friend Stephen Pemberly, whose father, the Earl of Weston, was away on the Continent:

MY DEAR WEYBOURNE,

I hope these few words find you hale and hearty, and coping well in these endlessly dreary days of winter. Mama and three of her friends have got it into their silly heads to have a Christmas-tide house party here at Rivercrest Hall, and I have been tasked to invite a couple of young, eligible bachelors in order to "make numbers," though I rather suspect she has a plan afoot to hogtie any and all of us to the young ladies who will also be in attendance. Got to make Mama happy, you know. I realise you're a busy man, but even God took some time off when He created the world, and perhaps you should, too. In any case, I picked up a fine new broodmare at Tattersall's and would like you to see her before we discuss my possibly breeding her to your Shareb-er-rehh. I also have some decisions to make about my own blood-stock, and beg the benefit of your advice and experience. Wine, women and horses...come to Rivercrest, Tristan. 'Twill do you good."

—*Stephen*

TRISTAN SIGHED AND LEANED ON HIS ELBOW, CHIN propped in his hand as he stared out the leaded glass windows of the library into a day as gray as the flesh of a dead fish.

Christmas here in Burnham Thorpe, most of the servants off with their own families, and only his horses, his business affairs and ventures and, if he were honest with himself, his loneliness to keep him company.

Or Christmas in Kent, with good old Stephen and a few silly young ladies who would be amusing and entertaining, even if he had no intention of marrying anyone until he had amassed a fortune equal to the amount he had squandered in his days of dissolution.

I don't have time to go to Kent.

There was too much here to be done. A proposal from a local landowner sitting on his desk waiting to be read. A tenant dispute down in the village that required his intervention. The damnable Amir, who needed a new groom.

I picked up a fine new broodmare at Tattersall's...would like you to see her...beg the benefit of your advice and experience.

Lord Weybourne sighed and rose to his feet. Going to Kent wouldn't be a slide into idleness after all. It would be talk of horses. The evaluation of horses. Work, after all.

Justified, if not excused.

He penned a reply, left the library and accepting the coat his valet held up for him, headed out to the stables.

IT HAD BEEN RAINING, OF COURSE.

The damp had seeped into the Norfolk soil to make a thick, sucking mud that claimed his boots up to the ankles. It was a miserable day, raw and damp just like the one before it, just like the one that would follow, the wind off the sea knifing into his bones and making him wish he'd added a layer of heavy wool beneath his greatcoat. Overhead, low clouds obscured any blue the sky might have offered, massing and swirling and lumbering out to sea.

Too bad they didn't take the damn rain with them.

He entered the stable and found the place in commotion.

"Now see here, laddie," said Mick, who had appointed himself in charge following Johnson's defection. The little Irishman had a shock of ginger hair long since thinned and going to gray, and freckles so thick across his sharp, clever face that a frog could have jumped them like lily pads. Mick wasn't a tall fellow, but he made the young lad standing next to him seem positively tiny.

"Now see here, what?" the young lad asked in a small voice. "I only wanted to see this colt I've 'eard so much about. The Norfolk Thoroughbreds are famous throughout England, they are."

"Famous or not, this is the private stable of the Earl of Weybourne. Ye can't come walkin' in here without invitation, ye can't! His Lordship owns some of the finest horseflesh in all of England, and these here are the fastest horses in the world. They're more valuable than every jewel in the king's crown, they are, and not just anybody can come in here and have a look at 'em, especially without invitation!"

Tristan had come up behind him, and sensing the master's shadow, Mick stiffened and turned. "Your Lordship!"

"What is the problem here, Mick?"

"Beggin' yer pardon, m' lord," the Irishman said, passing a frosty glare to the young lad who stood in the shadows nearby, "but I caught this little urchin here wanderin' the stables and lookin' at the horses. Asked him to state his business and he won't. I was just about to throw him out on his ear when you arrived."

Tristan straightened a bridle that was hung haphazardly on a peg. He leaned against the door of an empty box stall and eyed the young lad.

"What is your name?"

"Ledyard, m' lord."

"Is that your Christian or surname?"

"Either. Both. Only one I have."

"What the deuce kind of a name is that?"

The boy blushed beneath his oversized cap. "'Tis the name I was given, m' lord."

"Why did you come into our stable uninvited? This is highly irregular."

The boy hung his head and kicked at some loose straw at his feet. "I just wanted t' see the horses, m' lord.

I love horses, I do. My mistress was passin' through the area and I thought I'd take the opportunity to see a Norfolk Thoroughbred in the flesh." The kicking grew more agitated. "I never meant t' cause trouble. Just wanted to see the horses."

Tristan pursed his lips, thinking. There was something not quite right here, but he couldn't put his finger on it. Either way, the lad seemed harmless enough, and he knew plenty of horse-crazy youths. He'd been one himself. If the boy wanted to see a Norfolk Thoroughbred, what harm was there in granting him his wish and then sending him on his way?

"Very well, then, Ledyard," he said. "Come with me."

He glanced again at the young lad, his eyes narrowing, and began to walk toward Amir's stall.

"I'm in need of a groom, you know," he said offhandedly. Calculatingly. "You know how to rub down a horse, make a bran mash, bed down a stall?"

"I can do all that and then some."

"Can you ride?"

"Like the wind, m' lord."

"And are you afraid of young, nippy horses, the likes of which sent my last groom packing?"

"I'm not afraid of any horses, m' lord. Young ones, old ones, and everything in between ... none of 'em scare me."

Tristan stood eyeing the lad, his intense gray eyes narrowing in a sudden realization of just what had been niggling at him since he'd first spied Mick giving him a proper drubbing. *Of course.* But he would keep his suspicions to himself and let this game go where it may. The "lad" was no lad at all but a young lady, and judging by the fine bone structure and high cheekbones of her face, a very pretty one at that. But why on earth was she in disguise and what was she up to?

He'd find out. But for now, he'd play along with her little charade.

In Norfolk, in the dead of winter under an endless sky of damp gray cloud, there was little else to entertain a man anyhow.

He beckoned to Mick, who was sulking outside of the colt's stall.

"Let young Ledyard have a go with Amir," he said cheerfully, and turning his back, headed for the door to give them both a little space.

3

Dear God, what have I got myself into?

Letitia watched the Earl of Weybourne turn and walk away, feeling as though the very air had been sucked out of the space around her. Why was it suddenly so hard to breathe? Why did it feel as though someone was standing on her chest, and good Lord above, what had caused her skin to come alive with prickly sensation, her mouth to go dry and her palms to become suddenly damp? She felt breathless, hot, shivery, and warm in places she didn't know she had. Oh, heaven help her, he was a handsome one, the earl. The kind of man a young lady noticed.

Where have you been during my London Seasons, Lord Weybourne? Hidden up here in Burnham Thorpe?

She'd spent her life in Lincolnshire and her Seasons in London, and while he'd never graced a Season with his presence, she'd heard the rumors about him. Rumors that he was obsessed with his estate, making it run, breeding the horses that were his father's legacy. Not quite a recluse, but a man too busy and distracted to take a wife, to make himself available in Society, to meet and mingle with ladies on the marriage mart.

Stop thinking about Lord Weybourne and start thinking about the predicament in which you've found yourself!

Yes, she was in trouble, *deep* trouble this time, because this little venture to take a look at the son of the famous Shareb-er-rehh while giving herself time to think her way out of the Homer Trout Situation had landed her in yet another mess that she'd have to find a way out of. She ought to just bolt right here and now while she had the chance—before Beryl lost her nerve and went to Mama, before anyone back at Lady Ariadne's noticed her absence, before Lord Weybourne realized she was no lad and certainly not interested in joining his employ.

Oh, what a pickle she had got herself into this time!

"Want t' be a groom, do ye? Then go change out the water buckets and start earnin' yer keep," the abrasive Mick was muttering. He shoved a pail at her. "Ye can begin with Amir."

But Letitia was still watching Lord Weybourne retreating down the aisle, the broad shoulders clad in form-fitting dark gray wool, the breeches white as a dove's plumage, the shiny leather boots emphasizing the length of His Lordship's strong, muscled legs.

She felt a little flutter at the base of her sternum and wondered if her heart was jumping rope with itself.

"Did ye hear me, lad? I said t' start with Amir."

"Amir?"

"A-*meer*," he corrected, when her tongue tripped over the name. "Means 'prince' in Arabic. That little bugger is the spare to the heir, so t' speak. The Norfolk Thorough-breds are the fastest horses in the world, and this 'un's sire, Shareb-er-rehh, was the last o' the old earl's stallions. Sired another colt two years ago an' that one's got a disposition as kind as a summer day in Cork, but this one, oh, don't get me started. A throwback to that wretched desert blood, he is. Going t' kill someone if they're not careful. C'mon, hurry up, 'tisn't all day I have t' wait for ye. The well's outside, just beyond that door."

Letitia's mind was whirling, her hands clammy with rising anxiety as she gripped the handle of the bucket and ducked outside to find the well. She began to pump, willing herself to stay calm. To find a way out of this predicament as quickly as she could with no one the wiser. And oh, dear lord, there was Lord Weybourne standing at the other end of the building, in profile to her as he reached through a fence to stroke the forelock of a chestnut mare. Letitia's heart kicked up its beat and she forced herself to keep pumping when all she wanted to do was stop and stare at this splendid example of masculinity. She had more pressing matters to deal with than indulging herself with thoughts of Lord

Weybourne, but her heart was in hopeless rebellion. And so were her eyes, unable to look at anything else but the earl....

The water bucket overflowed, jarring her back to the present, and she slammed the handle down on the pump and hurried back into the stable, where she found the sour Mick waiting for her.

"Ye'll have to be faster than that if ye want t' impress His Lordship," Mick muttered, stalking down the neatly-swept aisle. "Hurry up, time's a' wastin'...."

Letitia glanced over her shoulder, hoping Lord Weybourne would come back. She was still reeling over the unexpected fact that he was so handsome, so personable, so ... virile. What would it feel like to be kissed by that firm, sensual mouth? What might his hair feel like beneath her fingers?

Horses. Look at the horses and stop thinking about him! She peered into the stalls as they passed each one. Here, a dark bay mare with a blaze ... there, a liver roan colt, obviously on his way to gray. Her eyes widened with appreciation, and she nearly plowed into Mick's back as he finally stopped behind a last stall containing a seal bay colt who could only be the notorious Amir.

"Watch him, 'e bites."

The colt stood behind the vertical bars of his door, nostrils pressed against the iron. Behind them, his dark eyes were flat and showed no emotion whatsoever. Letitia knew the look and she knew the ploy. Convince you into thinking they were bored or sad, convince you to put your hand in there.

Then say goodbye to your hand.

"Hello, Amir," she said.

The horse didn't move.

"I hear ye dine on people's fingers."

The colt lowered his eyelids a fraction of an inch.

"I know. Ye're trying to lull me into lettin' down my guard, aren't ye?"

The colt's lashes drooped a tiny bit more.

"Nasty little bugger, he is," Mick said sourly. "Not like his sire a' t'all." He handed her a lead rope. "Here. Take him out. Let's see if 'e takes to ye."

Yes, take me out, the colt seemed to say, never moving a muscle, his big, dark eyes still flat and hard. *If you dare.*

I dare.

Letitia hefted the lead rope in her hand and then she saw it. A tiny, barely perceptible twitch of the colt's ear in the direction of Mick.

"Can I 'ave some time alone with him?" she asked.

"What?"

"I—" She bit her lip. "I don't think 'e likes you."

Mick bristled. "He doesn't like anyone. And if I give ye time alone with him, there'll be nobody to pick up the pieces when he ends up killin' ye."

She held the colt's gaze, admiring his wide, intelligent forehead, his huge dark eyes and enjoying the feeling that she was standing with royalty. Somewhat dreamily, she murmured, "I don't think 'e'll kill me."

"Ye don't know this wretched beast," Mick said, frowning. "But I do, and I'm tellin' ye, he's—"

"Is there a problem here, Mick?"

Letitia gasped. Lord Weybourne had come back into the stable so quietly she had never even heard him and neither, apparently, had Mick, who looked suddenly uncomfortable. And sullen.

"Ledyard here wants me t' leave so he can take this wretched little monster out."

"If you stopped callin' him names," Letitia said quietly, "maybe 'e'd like ye better. He knows ye're afraid of him."

"I'm not afraid o' him!"

"He thinks you are."

"And ye're not?" the little Irishman shot back, hands on his hips.

"No." She reached out and gently, reverently, traced the shape of the colt's huge, velvety nostril through the bars of his stall. "I'm not."

She was aware of the fact that Lord Weybourne had moved closer to her. Closer than personal space dictated he should be, and she shivered. Did he suspect she wasn't the lad she pretended to be? Those penetrating gray eyes of his didn't look like the sort to be easily fooled.

Heat clawed its way up to her cheeks, reddening them, and she wished she dared pull off her cap so she could pass her sleeve across the back of her suddenly-damp brow.

"I have a commitment next week that begs both a degree of travel and my attendance," he said. "Not exactly an event I'm keen to attend, but it would give me far more pleasure to head off in the dead of winter over wretched, muddy roads if I could convince you to work for me instead of your present employer. I've not seen Amir react so favorably with anyone before, and I confess, I'm most impressed." He turned and smiled at the bristling little Irishman. "And you, Mick. Go take the afternoon off. I know your wife has been feeling poorly these past few days with a head cold. I'm sure she'll welcome your presence."

Mick brightened. "Why, thank ye, m'lord. Thank ye kindly, indeed."

"See you tomorrow."

The man ambled out, leaving a suddenly very breathless Letitia standing in the stable with Lord Weybourne.

Alone.

❦ 4 ❦

It was on the tip of her tongue to chastise him for standing so close to her, to rebuke him for putting her—a lady—in such a tenuous, reputation-shattering situation, but she remembered just in time that she was supposed to be a young lad, not a lady, and as long as Lord Weybourne still behaved as if she were a male and not a female, she would assume he knew no better.

"I like your manner around horses," he said, meeting her eyes. "Most of the young lads that have been hired to work here are terrified of Amir. He's the most valuable horse in this stable, the one on whom I'm pinning my hopes, and I can't have those to whom I'm entrusting his care and future running scared of him. It only makes him worse."

She turned away, unwilling to look for too long into his eyes for fear he'd guess her secret. "I only came here to see your famous horses, m' lord," she said quietly, hoping her nervousness, her racing heart, didn't show in her voice. "I'm loyal to my mistress. She treats me well, and I should get going before she misses me."

"I wish you would stay," he said. "Ledyard."

Something in the way he said her supposed name sent a prickle of fear up her spine. Did he know? Did he? Oh, she had to find a way out of here, and quickly!

He leaned against the stall door. "Do consider," he said. "If you stay, I'll give you charge of this colt. You would answer to me, not Mick or anyone else. He likes you. You like him. What do you say?"

"I cannot, m' lord."

Something in his face fell. He turned and slid back the bolt on Amir's stall and looked pointedly at the lead rope she still held in her hand. "Before you go, then, at least take a few moments to step into the stall with him. If nothing else, satisfy my own curiosity, Ledyard. I am keen to see how this young savage responds to someone who is truly not afraid of him."

She hesitated, at war within herself. The knowledge that she had to get out of this stable and this situation with pressing immediacy weighed on her, but oh, here was the chance to share space with the son of the famous Shareb-er-rehh, to experience royalty first-hand and, if her pride would admit it, to impress the handsome Lord Weybourne with her own confidence and abilities. Doing so served no purpose, of course, except to stroke her own pride and to add to memories that later, she could take out and treasure. This day of clandestine daring, of magic, of a few moments spent with both a Norfolk Thoroughbred and the unimaginably handsome Lord Weybourne....

She opened the door wide, stepped into the stall— and clamped her eyes shut as the colt struck out, teeth bared, as quick as a cobra and just as intentional.

The bite hit her hard, in the shoulder, though the fabric of her coat remained intact. The colt's head jerked up and back as he waited for her to take her hand to him in punishment.

She didn't move.

"Amir," she said softly, still not moving. "I will not harm ye."

Lord Weybourne stood quietly watching, not saying a word.

"Someone's been abusing 'im," she said. "He's testin' me. He bit me, then flung his head up, expectin' to be hit."

"He is about to bite you again."

She turned just as his bared teeth snaked toward her once again.

"Amir!" she said firmly.

The horse stopped, his eyes no longer flat and hard, but dangerous, angry and intentional. He *was* testing her. Trying to find her breaking point, the point where she would flee the stall, never to try again, and he would be left alone and unchallenged and chafing with unspent energy. This was a horse with plenty of spirit and plenty of fight—with those attributes properly channeled, she had no doubt that he might indeed prove himself to be the "fastest horse in the world."

"Ye don't frighten me, Amir."

She stood her ground as the colt, confused by her reluctance to show fear, to run for her life from his stall, lowered his head, his nostrils flared, squared, and quivering as he tried to discern what she was about.

Quietly, she extended her arm, palm up, and allowed him to slowly and purposely sniff her.

He raised his head. He was a striking colt, a dark seal bay with a thick, shaggy black mane and a forelock that tumbled down over his eyes. Powerful hindquarters. Long, strong legs, good layback of shoulder, a proud neck set on high. Intelligence and canniness in the eyes, small ears set atop a wide skull, big, flat cheekbones set wide apart to allow plenty of air to get to the great lungs that would power him.

"Ye're a glorious horse," she said, and smiled as the colt, one ear twitching back and forth, raised his head another inch ... closer to her hand ... and closer.

There.

Finally.

Velvet against the skin of her palm, the soft whiskers of his muzzle, the warmth of his breath.

The colt sniffed her hand, the wariness going out of his eyes, his head dropping an inch ... two.

"Ye can bite me over and over again, Amir," she said softly, as he took a hesitant step forward, pressing his muzzle against her hand, "but I'll never strike ye back."

She extended her fingers and gently scratched under the colt's jaw, smiling as he dropped his head another inch and moved a step closer. She looked up then and saw Lord Weybourne a few feet away, watching her with the intensity of a gun dog on a pheasant. He didn't say a word. Just stood there watching her, until heat began to bloom deep in the pit of her belly.

"I think," he said softly, "I have witnessed a miracle here tonight."

"No miracle," she said, looking away. "Just a horse who's desperate to find someone to stand up to 'im without hurtin' him, to not be afraid of him. He's smart."

"As are you, Ledyard."

There was something in his voice that made her head jerk up. "I beg your pardon, my lord?"

"What is your real name ... Ledyard?"

Alarm prickled the base of her spine and flooded her face, causing her to blush, and it was all she could do not to bolt. *He can never discover who I am, or my name will be ruined and my family will never survive the scandal!*

"Ledyard," she said with false affront.

But Tristan knew that she wasn't telling him the truth. He stood looking at her, a slow smile spreading across his face as he noted her increasing discomfort, her panic. The game was up.

"I think not," he murmured and reaching up, grasped her cap and pulled it off.

Thick, lustrous piles of golden-brown hair spilled down, fanning over her shoulders, tumbling down her back, and confirming what he knew to be true all along.

That she was a woman.

"Aha," he said thoughtfully, watching her sea-blue eyes go as wide as the perimeter of a tea cup. "And you thought you had me fooled ... Ledyard."

She swallowed hard, and he saw the panic growing in her eyes. She took a step back, out of the stall.

"I must go," she said, flustered.

His hand seized her wrist, staying her when she would have fled. "You are no lad, Ledyard. Why are you here, dressed as one?"

"I told you, I only wanted to see a real Norfolk Thoroughbred. Please unhand me."

"And you could not do that, dressed as a female?" He shut the stall door and stepped closer. "What are you running from, Ledyard?"

The girl looked him straight in the eye. "My mother," she said honestly. "And marriage to a man with a hair growing out of a nose-mole, a man to whom I'm to be thrown like a ball to a child if I don't find a way out of it. I needed to think. I think best on the back of a horse and when I'm around horses."

"And you could not do that, dressed as the lady I suspect you are?"

"I needed to sneak away from the household for an hour. That would be impossible dressed as my true self." Her chin came up a fraction of an inch as his smile spread. "Besides," she said mulishly, "I *did* want to see a real Norfolk Thoroughbred."

"And now you have."

"Now I have, and now I must go." She pulled free of his grip and moved out of the stall. He followed, intrigued. She was an enigma, this "Ledyard." Trying to pass herself off as a lowly, horse-crazy lad when she was, judging by her speech and her sudden poise now that the charade was over, most certainly of the upper classes. Or at least, associated with them. He wondered who her "mistress" was.

"You must go," he repeated. "You, the only person who has ever come into this stable and shown fearlessness and promise where Amir is concerned. The only person he has ever softened toward. And what do you wish to do, now that you've befriended my horse that hates everyone, now that you've charmed and intrigued me with your fearlessness and your ability?"

She kept walking, trying to put distance between herself and him. "Run away, I guess, before you discern who I really am."

"And I thought you were fearless." He caught up to her, quickly moved in front of her and stopped, so that she was also forced to halt or slam up against his chest. "I'd pay you well to stay, you know."

"That is absolutely out of the question."

"Surely this is a better deal than being married to a man you detest."

"It is. I'd sooner marry Amir. At least *he* doesn't have a mole growing out of his nose."

Tristan laughed. She said it with such earnestness, such a serious look on her face that he couldn't help himself, and with some surprise, he realized that it had been a long time, a very long time, since he had actually laughed so hard and with such pure and utter delight. He liked this sassy little miss. Of course she couldn't stay, not if she had a mama who was arranging a marriage for her, but nevertheless she intrigued him. And he was having a bit of fun teasing her and watching the play of emotion dance across her lovely face.

"So you reject my offer to stay," he said. And then, with sheer daring: "But before you leave, how about a kiss for me to remember you by?"

He hadn't thought that her eyes could go any wider.

"*What?*"

"A kiss." He smiled, enjoying her shock. "I did, after all, let you see the horses."

"I cannot kiss you!"

"Why not?"

"Because ... well...."

"Do you want to kiss me?"

"I can't answer that question. I am becoming distressed, the ruse is up, and I need ... I need to leave."

Tristan walked a little distance away, folded his arms and leaned against the smooth, varnished wood of an empty stall. "And here I thought you weren't afraid of anything."

"I'm not, except discovery and scandal."

"And me."

"I am not afraid of you!"

"Then prove it."

He saw the indecision in her eyes, the desire warring with panic, with desperation, and again, wondered who she was. Her skin had too many freckles from being out in the sunshine for her to be as well-bred as her speech would otherwise have marked her. Probably some vicar's daughter, or a governess fleeing a house where a hairy-moled gentleman lay in wait to ambush her.

He stepped forward, and when she didn't move, he reached out and drew her into his arms.

She made a faint sound of protest, but there was otherwise no fight in her. His hands cupped her jaw, his thumbs gently stroking her cheeks and forcing her to look up at him. He saw her throat move, the desire darkening her eyes as he pushed a hand into her lustrous fall of silken, glossy hair, relishing its thickness, its weight, its good health. He dragged his fingers through the thick, shining locks, down over her shoulders and into the curve of her back, there to press gently, to urge her closer to him. She moved shyly into his embrace, wide-eyed and unsure, but Tristan felt none of her uncertainty. She fit him like a well-tailored coat—just the right size, just the right shape, the top of her head coming up to just below his chin.

"Kiss me, Miss...."

"Lettie," she murmured a bit breathlessly, and he dropped his face into her hair. It smelled of lemons and summer long-gone, reminded him of primroses and sunshine and a happy, playful feeling that had long since abandoned his work-too-hard life that left no time for play, for joy, for simply kissing a very, very pretty young woman.

Their lips met. She was shy and inquisitive, hesitant but eager. She tasted like honey, her breath sweet and clean. He drew her closer, his hand splaying up her back, pressing her to him and desperately seeking more and more contact with her body. His mouth ground against hers, and she met his kiss with first hesitation and then abandon, her own hands now coming shyly up into his hair, her touch light, butterfly-like, maddeningly sensual.

He slipped his tongue out to tease apart her lips, and in that moment, she froze.

Oh, devil take it, he thought. He had frightened her.

She pulled back, her lips reddened from the kiss, her eyes wide. She was breathing hard, and as she took a step back, and then another, he saw that he had found the one thing that she was afraid of.

The response of her own body to a simple kiss.

She snatched up her hat, turned—and bolted.

Tristan watched her go, his spirits falling with every step she ran. He watched her splash through the puddles of sticky mud just outside the stables, watched her beautiful hair flying out behind her, and watched his hopes of getting to know the bold little miss disappear with every step she ran.

For a moment, he had forgotten his relentless pursuit of work. For a moment, his soul had felt light, free to float amongst the clouds with joyful abandon. And as he stood there, surprised by his reaction to this girl he knew only as "Lettie," Tristan St. Aubyn realized how very, very depressed he had actually become with his single-minded pursuit of a loveless goal, and how much his nose-to-the-grindstone work habits had cost him.

Were continuing to cost him.

He walked back down the aisle and saw Amir looking at him with that flat, dead look of abandonment, of a challenge issued and denied.

He reached out and stroked the colt's neck.

"Don't worry, I'll find her," Tristan vowed. "For both of us."

5

"And just where have you been, Letitia?" Mama asked, looking up from her embroidery and pinning her daughter from over the top of the spectacles she wore these days for close-work. "I was looking everywhere for you."

Letitia had returned to their host's home an hour before, darting in through the servant's entrance and dashing quickly back up to their rooms. Mama had not been there, and she'd taken advantage of that particular blessing to quickly employ a visibly nervous Beryl to put her back to rights. She'd found her mother downstairs in a parlor with her needlework. Mama did not notice that her hands were shaking, her lips puffy, her demeanor out of sorts. Thank the good Lord that her mother was so unobservant and wrapped up in her own affairs, Letitia thought. Still rattled by the dangers of her clandestine escapade, her nearness to getting caught and mostly, her meeting with the extraordinarily handsome Lord Weybourne, she did not feel as though she had enough wits left to do battle with her mother.

"I was with the horses," she said. "I needed some air." She sat in a nearby chair, shoving her hands between her knees and pressing her legs together to still their shaking. Her afternoon had brought excitement of a sort she hadn't bargained for, but she was no nearer to finding a way out of the Homer Trout Situation than she'd been when she'd impulsively ridden off. Perhaps it was time for her to just say what was on her mind. "Do we really have to go to this Christmastide house party, Mama?"

Her mother looked up. "I thought you were looking forward to it. To seeing your friends."

Letitia shrugged and looked out the window into the encroaching darkness. "It ... it is a long journey. I think I would just like to go back home to Lincolnshire."

"It is tradition, to visit our friends at Christmastime. We will attend."

Because you have plans for me. Plans that involve the odious Mr. Homer Trout.

"The roads will be bad, Mama. The coach, cold—"

"We will attend," her mother said again, looking up from her embroidery once more. Her eyes narrowed imperceptibly. "Is there a real reason you do not wish to go, Letitia?"

She could not tell her that the real reason involved

Mr. Homer Trout, because then Mama would know she'd been eavesdropping.

And she certainly could not tell her that the other real reason involved Lord Weybourne and the fact that his kiss had only enforced her conviction that she could never marry a man to whom she wasn't attracted, because then she would be in more trouble than a chicken plucked, parted, and plunged into boiling water.

Oh, what had she done?

"No," she said meekly, hanging her head so her mother might not see the truth in her eyes.

"I am glad to hear it. Now cheer up, Letitia. It is Christmastime, and I will not have such moroseness. Besides, one of your brothers might be there."

"Simon?"

"Yes. Lady Weston has numbers to make, so I have written to him. As his ship is currently in London, I expect he will be in attendance. Pity that Sheldon is out at sea ... I would like to see him there, as well."

"And Papa? Will he be there, too?"

"Perhaps, but probably not until Christmas Eve. He has not concluded his business in London."

Letitia turned away, not liking the perceptive way her mother was studying her face. "The fact that Simon may be there does not make the prospect of traveling all the way down to Kent in the dead of winter any more appealing," she said grumpily. Though truth be told, she was less enamored of the idea of seeing Homer Trout than she was of winter travel. And besides ... what man might she ever meet who could possibly compare to Lord Weybourne, and the strange, wonderful sensations he had aroused in her?

She had not been able to stop thinking of him.

He had spoiled her for anyone else.

She did not want to go.

"We will leave here and continue on our way first thing in the morning," her mother said with cheerful finality, returning her attention to her embroidery. She pushed the needle through the linen, pulled up a silken thread of bright yellow-gold, made an elegant and effortless knot and pushed the needle back down through the fabric once more. "There will be eligible bachelors at Lady Weston's party, and with several full days there to get to know each other I am hopeful that you will make a decent and respectable match."

Letitia went to the window and looked out into the cold, misty darkness, her fingertips digging into the recessed embrasure and her mind growing more and more desperate.

If Mama will not turn back and take us both home to Lincolnshire, then I have to think of a way to put Homer off once we get to this party.

"Letitia? Please go and dress for dinner."

"Yes, Mama." Sighing, she turned from the window, bent to give her mother a kiss on the cheek, and moved quietly from the room. *Oh, Lord, help me.*

A HOUSE PARTY.

A Christmastide house party.

Oh, why did I accept the invitation to go to this foolish, inane, sure-to-be-tedious thing? I have no time for this....

Tristan stood looking out over the flat Norfolk landscape as the day lightened through the copious cloud cover that was as integral to a British winter as fleas to a dog. He was depressed. Maybe if he were not, the crystalline beauty of everything covered in a hard, white frost might have stirred him to some sort of appreciation. Maybe if he actually enjoyed this season, he would be looking forward to seeing old friends and perhaps making some new ones down in Kent. God knew he had indeed been working hard.

But the girl in the stable....

He could not get her out of his mind.

It had been two days since she had come into his life, charmed the living devil out of Amir, shared a stolen kiss, and bolted, taking a piece of his heart with him. That, of course, was ridiculous in itself; he did not believe in love at first sight, and he knew nothing about her. Nothing.

And he still knew nothing except that she had made him feel things that he hadn't felt for years.

She had made him feel *alive*.

He had spent these past day combing the village and going door to door, describing her and receiving nothing but empty looks and helpless shrugs and offers of a glass of this or a glass of that to celebrate the season. One could get good and foxed on a glass of this or a glass of that, and Tristan, who felt more and more desperate, more and more in a race against time the longer his search went on and the more fruitless it became, was not inclined to get foxed.

And now here it was, time to leave for that blasted house party if he was going to go at all.

She had flitted into his life and flitted back out just like that, a sparrow on wings, and the confident determination that he would find her had given way to a morose acceptance that, in all likelihood, he would not ... and maybe never would. He could not get the memory of what she'd felt like in his arms, out of his head. The scent of her hair, the sweet pliancy of her mouth, the way she just seemed to *fit* him so perfectly....

"My lord?"

He looked up, bleary-eyed from lack of sleep. It was his valet, Ames. He responded with a raised eyebrow.

"Your coach has been readied, my lord. I have packed and loaded your trunks, and Cook has prepared a hot breakfast for you to eat on the way. Will you be wishing to leave soon?"

"Yes, best to get an early start."

Ames bowed and went out but Tristan remained standing there, gazing morosely out over the back garden, at the pastures enclosed by hedgerows and fencing, all frozen beneath the night's deposit of white crystals. It would be a long, muddy, cold trip down to Kent and he wasn't looking forward to it. Or pretending to be happy and full of "cheer" in a house stuffed with dull strangers and twittering young women looking for husbands, when he could think of nothing but the girl who had run away from him.

He wished he could cry off.

He'd far rather just stay home.

※ 6 ※

"**O**h, Lenore—I am so glad you were able to make it. I know the roads down from Norfolk must have been positively awful!"

No sooner had Letitia and her mother, accompanied by their maids, arrived at Rivercrest Hall than the great doors to the mansion had swung open and Lady Weston herself was rushing across the foyer to greet them. If she had a sly and knowing smile for Lady Penmore, Letitia did not see it; if speaking glances were exchanged over her shoulder while she and her godmother embraced, she wasn't aware of it. Servants had already whisked away their coats and hats, ferried their trunks upstairs, and Lady Weston was calling for tea before either Letitia or her mother could shake the cold from their bodies and gaze around the great hall in relief that they had finally arrived.

Lenore was excited and chattering, exchanging small talk with their hostess about the weather, their absent husbands, the roads down from Norfolk, and what was planned for this house party. Letitia, still thinking of Lord Weybourne and dreading the prospect of seeing Homer Trout, heard little of it. "You won't have a moment to get bored," Lady Weston was saying as they all walked down a corridor toward a drawing room. "The other guests are already beginning to arrive and tonight, I have a wonderful dinner planned where we'll all have the chance to get to know each other. Why—"

"Will Homer Trout be there?" asked Letitia, no longer caring that Mama might put two and two together and realize she'd been eavesdropping back at Lady Ariadne's home in Norfolk.

"Who?"

"Homer Trout."

Her mother grabbed Lady Weston's arm. "Homer Trout. You know him, Agatha! He was most interested in my Lettie last year, nice fellow, very well connected and in line to inherit—"

"Oh, yes, *that* Homer Trout!" said Lady Weston a little too brightly, and Letitia frowned in confusion and glanced from one to the other as they continued down the huge hall. "Why, I do believe he'll be arriving sometime tomorrow, most charming young man if I do say so myself!"

Lady Weston and her mother exchanged another

glance, and something niggled at the base of Letitia's spine. Panic. These two were planning something.

Or hiding something.

Jane. She was Lady Weston's daughter, also a Season Failure after failing to catch a husband. Jane would know what was going on here.

"Where is Jane?"

"Why, she's in the Blue Drawing Room with Pru," Lady Weston said happily, referring to Lady Prudence Carmichael. "Winnie is not here yet, but should arrive shortly." The knowledge that the four of them—friends since forever—would all be here together for this house party cheered Letitia considerably; if anyone could help her escape the attentions and mole hair of Homer Trout, it was her friends. "Why, I do believe the three of them have been awaiting your arrival for the past hour!"

Letitia looked to her mama for approval to go seek her friends, was given a brief, austere nod, and hurried off, leaving Lenore gazing after her until she was safely out of sight.

The viscountess waited until she heard a distant door shut. Then she looked at her friend Agatha, the Countess of Weston, and began to giggle like a schoolgirl.

"Homer Trout?" said Agatha, brows raised. "Honestly, Lenore, *what* were you thinking?!"

"I was thinking that Lettie would be so horrified by the idea of him being here that she'd take an interest in one of our eligible bachelors in the hopes of finding herself affianced before Homer arrives," she replied, trying to keep her laughter under control.

"She does not know that the esteemed Mr. Trout married an Essex girl and is settled happily at his modest estate in Dover?"

"No, and if she finds out, my schemes will be for naught." It was then that Lenore noted the excitement in her friend's face. "But you're hiding something yourself, Agatha. I've known you for enough years that that sparkle in your eye can only mean one thing. You have news."

"I do indeed."

Lenore raised a brow, waiting.

"I will let Pamela tell you. Ah, here she comes, now!"

Footfalls sounded in the hall and the other two mamas, Lady Carlisle and Lady Portland, came forward, arms extended. Embraces were exchanged, appearances remarked upon (favorably, of course), the weather discussed, and with the lot of them happy and excited and feeling as devilish and naughty as they once had when they'd pulled a prank on the autocratic Mrs. Brickhouse back in finishing school, headed for a drawing room of their own.

"So," Lenore said, touching Lady Portland's plump white arm, "Agatha says you have something to tell us?"

"I do." She pushed open the door to the study. "The handsome Lord Trent Ballantine seems to have captured my Winnie's heart. Unless I miss my guess, he'll be offering for her before this party is over."

"One down, three to go," said Clare, the Marchioness of Carlisle.

Agatha grinned. "And the party has barely started."

Lenore, all too aware of her daughter's keen ears and tendency to eavesdrop, shut the door behind them.

"Are the young gentleman beginning to arrive?" she asked, accepting a cup of tea from Agatha as she took a seat by the fire.

"In droves," Pamela said. "Your son Simon sent word ahead that he'll be here later this afternoon and may bring one of his lieutenants with him ... one can always count on the Royal Navy to deliver. Who else is already here, Agatha?"

"Lord Athmore, brooding and quiet as usual, but ever so handsome. Christopher Chance, who is still *insisting* that he's not a pirate."

Lenore's eyebrow went up. "Is he not?"

"No, he has a letter of marque, of course."

"Oh, dear," said Lenore, thinking of her upstanding son, a Royal Navy captain who would not take kindly to a supposed pirate being in their midst. "That won't hold much water with my dear Simon. We must endeavor to keep them away from each other so that we don't have a naval battle out in your pond, Agatha."

"It's frozen at the moment."

"The lord be praised," added the pious Clare.

"Anyone else coming?"

Agatha settled back with her own tea, blowing gently across its surface to cool it somewhat. "My Stephen tells me that he's invited a friend of his who breeds horses. A young, wealthy friend whose opinion he's seeking on that new mare he bought at Tattersall's. Stop grinning like a fool, Lenore, you know perfectly well who it is as it was by *your* insistence that he was invited!"

"Mine and his sister's," Lenore said, stirring her tea. "One must not forget she is a part of this, too."

"A bachelor?" asked Pamela, perking up.

Agatha reached for a biscuit. "Indeed."

"Titled?" asked Clare.

"An earl."

Lenore lifted her teacup, her eyes bright and laughing above its rim. Her decision to spend the night at Lady Ariadne's home instead of a local inn on the way down to Kent had not been purely a social call but a way to firm up some plans they had both been making. Letitia wasn't the only one under subtle manipulation by a well-meaning family member....

"Do tell Clare and Pamela who this young gentleman *is*, Agatha."

"Tristan St. Aubyn," their hostess replied. "The very handsome, very unattached, and very eligible Earl of Weybourne, who took over after his father's death as breeder of the Norfolk Thoroughbred ... the fastest horses in the world."

Clare turned to Lenore. "Oh, he sounds *perfect* for your Lettie!"

"Yes, his sister Lady Ariadne and I were of the same mind," Lenore allowed, sipping her tea. "I only hope that he has accepted the invitation to this little party of ours, as he seems disinterested in anything but horses, business ventures, and running his estate."

"A driven man, by all accounts," said Pamela.

Clare crumbled a biscuit on her plate. "Has to be, given what a cock-up he made of his life in his younger days."

"But a most eligible bachelor now."

"Yes, *most* eligible, indeed."

Lenore was persistent. "And did he accept?"

Agatha grinned. "He did."

Lenore set down her teacup, consumed by a fit of giggles. "Oh, Agatha," she murmured, dabbing at her lips with her napkin. "This is going to be the *best* Christmas party ever." Her eyes sparkled with warmth and delight. "And just when is he supposed to arrive?"

At that moment, there was movement beyond the great windows that overlooked the front garden, a flash of color and the thunder of a well-matched team, and Lady Weston put down her own teacup.

"Why, Lenore, I believe he just did."

TRISTAN PERSONALLY OVERSAW THE STABLING OF HIS team, watching in quiet approval as the Weston grooms unhitched the two matched blacks, rubbed them down, and set them up with bran mash and hay in adjoining stalls. He shivered and rubbed his hands together, trying to generate some warmth. Outside, the weather had turned cold, gray, and raw. While there was warmth awaiting him in the big house itself, he would have been quite happy to linger here in the stable for another hour ... or two ... or more, despite the cold. The long trip down from Norfolk over muddy, rutted roads had taxed his energy and his spirits, reminding him of all the work he could have been doing had he stayed home, reminding him of his loneliness ... and reminding him of the distance that was now between himself and the girl back in Norfolk, her identity still a mystery he intended to solve.

And now he would be expected to make conversation, participate in what was likely a full schedule of dull and boring activities, and flirt with or even offer for one of the young ladies that Stephen said would be in attendance.

Stephen, who had a broodmare he wanted Tristan's opinion on.

And it couldn't have waited until spring?

"Mama needs to make some numbers on her house party," Stephen had written, when a reply to his first note hadn't been immediately forthcoming. *"You're up there rattling*

around in that old pile of yours, Tristan. Come on down to Leeds in Kent, make some merry, meet some ladies, and see this mare of mine. You know you want to...."

What he *knew* was that he had a ton of things left undone back home, and being here at this ridiculous house party was the last thing he ought to be doing.

I don't have time for this. I really don't.

But he was here now, and he could not spend the next few days hiding out here in the stable, no matter how appealing he found the idea compared to the activities and expectations that surely awaited him inside River-crest Hall over the next few days.

Satisfied that the horses were being well cared for and suddenly overcome by a deep and resigned weariness, Tristan turned, and wanting nothing more than rest and a hot bath before the party kicked off with tonight's planned dinner and entertainment, headed for the house.

He had several hours before he'd be expected to be witty, charming, engaging and presentable.

He intended to make good use of them.

7

"You will wear the rose silk for the dinner this evening, Letitia," said her mother in a tone that brooked no argument. "It goes better with your complexion than the lavender."

"But I like the lavender."

"Be that as it may, the lavender does not like you."

Letitia's mouth grew mulish.

"If you are to make a worthy match, you should set your coloring off to its best advantage, not sabotage yourself with a color that makes you look sallow."

"Mama, you don't understand current fashions. You ... are of a different time and place."

"Are you saying, my dear, that I am—" she smiled, lips quivering with suppressed laughter—"old?"

"Of course not! But fashion has changed since you

were my age, and lavender is a popular color amongst my set. I wish to wear it."

Her mother stood there for a long moment, not saying a word. Then she gave a dramatic sigh and tilted her jaw as she studied her daughter. "Very well, then. Wear the lavender. If you like it so much then it's sure to give you confidence, and if you're to net Mr. Homer Trout, then confidence is the name of the game. Yes. Yes, do wear the lavender after all ... what was I thinking?"

She swept out of the small attached dressing room to Letitia's bedroom, leaving her daughter frowning.

Mama is behaving very strangely. Something is going on here and I wish I could put my finger on it.

She had discussed the matter at length with her friends Prudence, Winnie, and Jane, who was so starry-eyed in love with the all-too-quiet but intriguing Lord Athmore that her mind was of little use in helping to figure a way out of the Homer Trout Situation. But Winnie and Pru also sensed that something was up, and the three of them had pledged to be on their guards during the upcoming meal that was to be the great opener to this Christmastide house party.

Rose versus lavender.

One that flattered her complexion or one that was guaranteed to repel?

In the end, she decided against them both, and went with a soft apple-green tied under the bosom with a simple band of French lace.

"A perfect choice, m'lady," said her maid, Beryl. "It sets off the gold in your hair."

"I'm not sure I wouldn't have been better off setting off the brown," she said ruefully, because the last thing she wanted to do was make Homer Trout sit up and take notice of her.

The green was a good compromise. A quiet but unmistakable defiance of her mother's wishes, and yet not downright suicidal like the lavender.

She smiled, dabbed a bit of lavender water on her wrists and behind her ears, and went to find her mother.

She'd gotten lavender in after all.

A BEAUTIFUL ROOM OF PANELED WALLS AND DAMASK hangings, ancient portraits in gilt frames, glimpses as he stood in the small crush waiting to be announced into the dining room, of a long table that glittered with silver, china and crystal. Boughs of evergreen on a mantel, laughter, and people in beautiful clothes already taking their seats. The day had been gray, the night chilly and damp but here inside, the candles burning in a great chandelier overhead, in sconces on the walls, and on the table, the warm glow lent an ambience to the setting that was festive and welcoming. As he peered over the glittering gold epaulets of a Royal Navy captain who was coldly assessing the dark-haired man whom his friend

Stephen was engaging in conversation nearby, Tristan resisted the urge to pull out his watch.

I don't have time for this, he thought for the twentieth time this hour.

It was going to be a long night.

Around him came the sound of voices, feminine laughter, the low buzz of conversation, more laughter. People were in jovial spirits with the exception of the naval captain, who was coldly raking Stephen's friend with a visual broadside meant to sink. Maybe this evening would promise more entertainment than what might have been scheduled by the hostess, Tristan thought wryly.

"The Marquess and Marchioness of Carlisle."

The butler's voice droned on, and the milling crush in which Tristan was caught took a few steps closer to the great double doors to the dining room. He found himself engaged in idle small talk with Stephen's friend, the tall, dark-haired fellow the naval captain had now pointedly turned his back on—"believes all that drivel that I'm a pirate, he does ... Christopher Chance, glad to make your acquaintance"— and noted the twittering giggles of two young ladies trying to observe him, unnoticed, over their fans. The smell of something delicious was coming from the dining room. He found his attention drifting, even as his stomach sent up a plaintive growl that was drowned beneath the din around him. He was in no hurry to be announced; his bored pose and tamped-down urge to pull out his watch was not pretense, but a helpless reflection of how he felt. There was a slow, nagging pain building at the base of his skull, and he began to crave fresh air.

Two hours, maybe three. That's all the time I'll need to invest in this tedious thing before we get to repair to some library for brandy and cigars. Two meager hours. I can do this.

For the hundredth time since he'd set out from Norfolk, he wondered why he was here. Surely, it wasn't just to see Stephen's new horse, or to make Lady Weston happy by adding to the number of eligible bachelors. It was no secret that he was an eligible bachelor, but Tristan was hard-pressed to name any marriages—aside from the one his sister and her veterinarian-husband, Colin, enjoyed—that yielded happiness, mutual contentment, and an abiding, enduring, ever-growing love.

You put so much into the estate, your inheritance, the Norfolk Thoroughbreds. Don't you owe it to them to take a wife? To fulfill the requirement you owe that inheritance?

Maybe, in some way even he could not acknowledge, he'd come here hoping to find a wife ... even though he did not want a marriage based on necessity, practicality and the continuation of a family line, as so many *ton* marriages were. He did not want to pick out a wife the same way he would select new bloodstock for his farm; checking the teeth, assessing the physical beauty, determining intelligence and in the case of a prospective mate, her suitability for running his household. Most of the twittering bird-brains to whom he'd been introduced since he'd inherited the title had him bored within ten minutes, in almost physical pain after twenty, and he could not imagine spending his life shackled to such a person.

No, when he married, it would be to a woman who shared his passions, his interests, and whose strengths and weaknesses complemented his own.

He wanted a marriage like Ari had with her beloved Colin.

Damn, damn, damn about that little lad who'd turned out to be an elusive female. He'd give his eyeteeth—hell, he'd even give Amir—to find out who she was. She was unique, spirited, intriguing, and she'd made him laugh. She loved horses. In his very bones, he knew that they would have had a lot of fun together, that life with one such as her would never get old, or dull, or unhappy....

"The Earl and Countess of Portland, Viscount Munthorpe, and Lady Winifred Grisham."

The press moved closer to the door. Discreetly, he pulled out his watch and was just glancing at its face when again he heard feminine laughter coming from one of a group of young ladies about to enter the dining room. He looked up to peruse its source just as its owner, seemingly partnered with Captain Cold Eyes and chaperoned by an attractive woman of middle years, turned to look over her shoulder at the people milling behind her....

Tristan dropped the watch.

Their gazes collided across fifteen feet of space, past a half-dozen hungry guests waiting to be announced, and held.

Breeches and a cap hiding glorious honey-brown hair … pert, lively sea-blue eyes, a full and impish mouth, and memories of a kiss that had not left him since she'd fled the stable in distant Norfolk.

No.

It couldn't be.

But by the shocked, wide-eyed look in her eyes and the stunned "O" to her mouth, he knew that it was.

"Viscountess Penmore, Captain Simon Ponsonby, and the Honourable Miss Letitia Ponsonby."

Letitia.

Ledyard

Lettie.

And then *she*, still staring wide-eyed at him, was pulled through and out of their shared and momentary trance and into the dining room, leaving him feeling as though he'd just been kicked in the chest, his heart fighting to regain its beat, his lungs to reclaim their air.

His pulse grew loud. Louder. So loud that he no longer heard the small crowd around him, the laughter from within and without, the chime of a clock somewhere off to his right. He retrieved his watch. His head buzzed with delighted shock and he suddenly forgot that he was bored, that he was lonely, that he had no time to be here and that this was the last place in the world that he wanted to be.

In that moment, it became the *only* place in the world that he wanted to be.

He became downright impatient to get into that room, to be near *her*, to make his claim on her from the naval captain ... what had they said his name was? Did it matter?

Lady Letitia Ponsonby.

That was the only name that mattered.

"The Earl of Weybourne."

The butler's announcement shook him from his racing thoughts, kicked up his heartbeat even more, made a flutter of anticipation dry the back of his throat. He wiped suddenly damp palms on his coattails, made an unnecessary adjustment to his stock and walked boldly into the room.

No.

Yes.

He was being directed to the empty seat beside her, the seating arrangement male, female, male, female....

Oh, *yes*.

He took his seat, leaned back as a footman splashed sparkling wine into his glass, and looked at the young woman beside him.

"The Honourable Miss Letitia Ponsonby, eh?" he murmured, with a slow, warm smile meant to disarm. By the sudden flush that started at the base of her throat and spread upward to the roots of her hair, he knew he'd been successful in doing just that. "It is good, very good, to meet you again ... *Lettie*. Though this is the last place I expected to find an errant lad whom I've spent the better part of the last week trying to find."

She was battling to control her blush, now grabbing at her fan and beating it madly to direct air toward her face. "You were looking in the wrong place, my lord."

"Why did you run off?" he demanded, for her ears alone. "Why did you not tell me who you were?"

"Because if you knew who I was and word got out, my reputation would have been in shreds."

"Gentlemen never tell."

"I think I ... need some fresh air," she said, flustered.

"And do you know what I think?"

She swallowed hard and her fan beat a little faster.

"I think this dreary, boring house party just got a whole lot more interesting by the very fact that you're here and part of it."

On her opposite side the naval captain, his thick, glossy hair stylishly cut and hopelessly tousled, turned to look at Tristan with a penetrating gaze that could cut through fog. "I don't believe I've made your acquaintance," he said tersely. "Though it is obvious that you have made my sister's."

His sister. Relief washed over him. *Sister.*

Thank God.

"Ah, you heard that, did you?" Tristan murmured, caught.

"Keen hearing is a family trait."

Tristan reached around behind the lady's back and extended his hand. "Tristan St. Aubyn," he said.

The naval captain's grip was hard and firm, and a taciturn smile broke the tanned hardness of his face. "Simon Ponsonby." His gaze cut to the back of his sister's head and then to Tristan's once more. "I am sure we have a lot to ... discuss."

The implication was clear. Based on what he'd just heard, Ponsonby thought he'd played fast and loose with his sister's honor and was expecting him to either meet him at dawn with swords or pistols—or make an offer for her.

The lady herself turned to look at her brother, her eyes wide as she also caught the implication. "Simon!" she whispered fiercely. "It's not what you think!"

"Is it not?"

Tristan took a sip from his wine glass. "Do not distress yourself, Miss Ponsonby. I will be quite glad to discuss certain matters with your brother. Perhaps after dinner, Captain?"

The officer gave him a level stare. "You may depend on it."

Tristan inclined his head in assent. Permission to court the girl. They'd discuss that, and nothing more. At least, not yet. But would that be enough for

Ponsonby? He didn't need to make an enemy of the man, though in that moment the bright eyes of Lady Penmore, so like her daughter's, met his from across the table and he saw the laughter brimming in their depths.

"You must excuse my son," she said, as one of several liveried footmen now serving the table placed the first course before her. "He forgets that battles really should be confined to the sea."

The naval captain might have rolled his eyes, but even he was not beyond the reach of maternal authority, and he raised his glass in a wry little toast to his mother before turning his silent, assessing gaze on Christopher Chance, the rumored pirate, who was seated a ways down the table.

He might have let the matter go, but his mother did not. Lady Penmore's approach was altogether different from her son's, though her objective was obviously the same.

"So it seems that the two of you have met," she continued, eyeing Tristan with a mixture of assessment, delight, and cunning observation that she quickly masked with an overly open smile. "And where might that have been? I do not recall you being around for any of the recent Seasons."

"Indeed, my lady, I have not been."

"Why not?"

Tristan's gaze met hers across the table. Boldness and

direct questioning seemed to be a hallmark of this family, and it was actually quite refreshing.

He could give her the same respect.

"I have not been in the market for a wife."

"And are you now?"

"Mama!" hissed her daughter, going red with embarrassment once more.

"I confess that it was not my intent to look for one when I accepted this invitation," Tristan said carefully, wishing he could discreetly reach out and grasp Miss Letitia's hand beneath the tablecloth in reassurance and simply for the pleasure of touching her, "but a fellow's intentions are always subject to change."

She smiled, the gesture hinting at the cunning he'd glimpsed a moment ago, so briefly shown and so quickly disguised. He hoped to God she wouldn't ask again how he and her daughter had met, because he'd pointedly not answered the question. If she did persist, he'd be obligated to tell the truth to one as discerning as he perceived Lady Penmore to be, and this was a situation that could quickly spiral out of his control if he were not careful.

Especially with her son the naval captain just waiting for him to make a misstep.

He was not in the market for a wife. He was too busy, and he didn't have time to put down the relentless pursuit of amassing a fortune to court one—though in this instance, an exception could be granted. God knew he hadn't been able to think of much else besides the woman he'd known only as "Lettie" anyhow, since that brief encounter in his stable....

She was looking down at her plate, pushing the food around with her fork. None of it had made its way to her mouth. How mortified she must be, after the exchange that had just ensued.

"So where is your Man with the Mole?" he murmured for her ears alone, and his cajoling tone had the desired effect of taking her mind off the recent conversation, of which she was the subject.

"Oh, do not remind me of my plight! I have been wondering for the past few days what I can do to discourage his attentions once he arrives." She made a little noise of desperation. "He is supposed to be here tomorrow. Mama has great plans for the two of us."

I have better ones.

"You are very beautiful, Miss Letitia. I predict he will fall in love with you and sweep you off your feet."

She blushed all over again, but her eyes sparkled and she pursed her lips in a way that made him want to kiss them into open, parting submission. "I do not quite know what to say to such a complement, sir."

"'Thank you' would be a start."

"Thank you, then."

"And 'yes, Lord Weybourne, I would love to take you up on your offer to go riding tomorrow so as to escape the attentions of Man with the Mole.'"

"But you have not asked me to go riding."

"I was getting to that."

"Well, even though you have not asked, but are getting to that, then I feel compelled to give you my answer which, of course, is yes." She glanced at her mother, who was conversing with Lady Weston, and lowered her voice. "How is Amir?"

"He misses you. Tore a chunk out of Mick's arm after you left." He leaned close, catching a whiff of her delightful fragrance—lavender. "You should not have run away, Letitia."

"I ... have not given you permission to use my Christian name."

"I'm sorry." He put his head to one side and smiled, his eyes twinkling. "Ledyard."

"*Shh!*"

"Does your mama have the same keen hearing that you and your brother share?"

"Where do you think we got it from?"

"So are you looking forward to going riding with me tomorrow? We can put the slip on Man with the Mole."

She laughed and took a sip of her wine. "Mama will be cross if she thinks I'm making a scandal when she has all but promised me to him."

"Perhaps, Miss Letitia, a little scandal is just what is needed to frighten him off."

"Perhaps," she said slowly, her smile spreading, "you are correct." And then, her eyes sparkling, "Would you be willing to help me create just a bit of a scandal, Lord

Weybourne? A perfect Christmas scandal, so that Mr. Homer Trout will decide that I am not the woman for him after all?"

"I would be delighted," he murmured, letting his gaze drink in the beauty of her face, and he wished he could reach out and caress that pert upper lip, the full and pink lower one or better yet, claim those smiling lips with his mouth ... his tongue. God, she was beautiful. How on earth had he let her get away from him back in Norfolk?

"Homer arrives tomorrow. Meet me downstairs, early, and by then I will have thought of something."

8

The main course was fish garnished with slices of lemon—flaky, perfectly cooked, and perfectly wasted on Letitia, who was aware of nothing but the fact that the handsome Lord Weybourne was here, in Leeds, at *this* Christmastide house party.

And sitting next to *her*.

Yes, there was fish, as well as winter vegetables and rolls and mince pies and wine, lots of wine. There was a fire in the hearth, mistletoe on the mantel, the smell of evergreen and burning wax and the warm glow of candlelight reflecting off the great windows that held back the darkness outside. Laughter, toasts, someone who'd imbibed a little too much doing a drunken rendition of God Rest Ye Merry Gentlemen, Winnie spilling her drink and being swept off her feet by the sudden, unexpected, and outrageously romantic entrance of Lord Trent Ballantine with a proposal of marriage. But Letitia was only dimly aware of it all. For her, there was only Tristan St. Aubyn and the deliciously warm tingles that skated over her flesh at his nearness, the sound of his deep voice, the occasional discreet brush of his fingers against her own beneath the tablecloth. He was talking about something—horses, she thought—but she was only half-aware of what he was saying, instead thinking about the way his auburn hair had a rakish insouciance about it that mirrored his very character, studying the little crinkles at the corner of his intense gray eyes when he answered Mama's questions, and wondering if he, like she, was dreading the one question she was sure Mama was going to make inevitable.

"So tell me again, Lord Weybourne, how did you and my Lettie meet?"

Leave it to Mama not to disappoint.

Letitia's stomach dropped somewhere down beneath the level of her hips and bounced back up again, taking her heart with it into her throat, but Lord Weybourne countered it with smoothness and ease.

"We met over horses, Lady Penmore."

"I see." Mama's fork dropped to the lemon on her fish, pushed it gently aside with a barely perceptible flick of the tines, and sank into the tender white flesh. "And where was that, my lord?"

Beside her, the earl smiled and said genially, "Do you really wish to know, Madam?"

Letitia nearly choked on her own fish. Tristan St. Aubyn had bottom, that's for sure, to be challenging her mama so, but she also saw the *touché* in her mother's smile and knew that Mama appreciated Weybourne's attempts to not only safeguard her reputation, but to go hand to hand with her in a clandestine battle of wits.

"Perhaps," Mama said, smiling, "we will revisit this topic later. And in private."

"As you wish."

"As I would wish, too," put in Simon from Letitia's left, and she realized that he'd been listening to this exchange in his silent, observant way, choosing to add to it only when it suited him or he could get in a salvo of his own.

Which was good.

Anything to have her brother's keen attention on her and Tristan as opposed to Christopher Chance, currently exchanging warm exchanges and conversation with Pru just down the table. Oh, she'd heard the rumors all night —that the man was a pirate, something gone wrong with his supposed letter of marque, and to have one such as he in the same room as a Royal Navy captain who did everything by the book ... no, this could not end well.

An accidental brush of Lord Weybourne's thigh against her own as he shifted position in his seat reclaimed her attention. The devil take Simon. And Christopher Chance, too.

I still cannot believe he *is here.*

Here.

Memories of that hot and forbidden kiss they'd shared in his stables flashed into her mind and goose-bumps rose on her arms. She shuddered.

"Are you cold, Miss Ponsonby?"

"No, quite the opposite," she said truthfully, but nevertheless adjusted her light silken shawl over her shoulders. *Cold?* With him sitting next to her?

"So I understand you raise horses," Mama was saying. "What a small world! Your sister Ariadne is a friend of mine. In fact, Lettie and I stayed with her and Colin on our way down here to Kent." She refolded her napkin in her lap and looked up, directly into Lord Weybourne's eyes, her own gleaming above a disarming smile. "I understand you live quite near to her?"

Letitia gulped. Oh, no. Mama had picked up the scent like a hound on a trail.

"Very near, Madam."

Mama said nothing and just nodded once, with a tiny, self-satisfied little smile, and Letitia wanted to squirm in her chair.

"My sister and I share the horses and my father's lega-cy," Lord Weybourne continued, cutting a piece of fish and dragging it through the juices that bathed the bottom of his plate. "It's been a long road following my father's death and the loss of almost the entire herd of Norfolk Thoroughbreds." Letitia's gaze dropped to his hands, watching them as they wielded knife and fork and went about the business of getting food from his plate to his mouth. She wondered if he could sense the rapt attention she was paying the shape of them, the way the knuckles and tendons came together just beneath his tanned skin, his short, perfectly manicured nails. If only she'd had time to touch those hands, to explore them, when they'd last met....

"How many horses are left?" Simon asked from her left.

"We have our herd stallion, Shareb-er-rehh. The last original mare, Gazella. A three-year-old colt with the sweetest of dispositions and a yearling colt with the most sour. We were hoping for a filly this year, but Gazella came up barren."

Down the table, the Marchioness of Carlisle, known to be a religiously prudish sort, blanched as she caught the tail end of Tristan's sentence. "My goodness," she said disapprovingly. "Such conversation, and at the dinner table as well!"

"Don't you like horses, Lady Carlisle?" asked Letitia, before Lord Weybourne could fashion a response.

"I like them from the interior of a coach. I like them in paintings on my wall. I do not care to discuss their procreation."

"My dear Clare," cut in Letitia's mother smoothly, "do

you not remember the match race from four years back? When the Weybourne's horse defeated that monster, Black Patrick?"

"I do not follow horse racing."

It was Prudence, still exchanging secret glances with Christopher Chance, who jumped in to save the day before it could deteriorate further. "Isn't this fish marvelous, Mama?" she asked, with a sly wink at Letitia. "I do hope Lady Weston's cook will be persuaded to share the receipt!"

After that the evening settled somewhat, with talk moving from fashion, the Prince Regent, the weather, the deplorable state of the roads heading into Leeds, and of course the meal, which was spectacular in every way. Letitia noticed that Lord Weybourne didn't initiate much conversation, though she *did* notice that he watched her when he thought she wasn't looking, that he made sure she had plenty of food on her plate and that her glass was constantly full, and that he was most solicitous of her in every way. She knew that if he was dying to talk about anything, it wasn't the weather, the meal, or the Regent.

It was horses.

A conversation she was eager to share with him.

THE DINNER CONCLUDED, THE MEN RETIRED TO THE library for spirits, smokes, and politics, and the women gathered for tea. After the four daughters had each had a cup, Lady Weston ushered them all out of the room with the excuse that the hour was late and there was much planned for the following day.

"We can't have you girls looking tired tomorrow after such a long night," she said firmly.

"Indeed," added Lady Portland, "you'll want to be fresh and rested. Lots to do tomorrow!"

Protesting, the four younger women said their good-nights and left the room as a group.

"Are they gone yet?" asked Lady Penmore.

"Of course they are, Lenore," said Lady Carlisle with a casual wave of her hand. "You just saw them go."

"I know my daughter," she murmured, and rising, moved silently to the door. With the other three women watching, she yanked it open. On the other side was a startled Letitia, who jumped back into the arms of her three friends in alarm.

"I knew it," said Lady Penmore. "Get to bed, all of you."

"Mama, I wasn't eavesdropping, I was just coming back because I— I forgot my shawl!"

"Of course you were. Your shawl is on your shoulders. Now get to bed."

Grumbling, the young ladies moved off down the hall,

only Letitia looking back over her shoulder and trying to convince her all-too-knowing mama of her innocence.

Lenore waited until their footsteps had faded, then shut the door firmly behind her.

The four mamas all took seats in a horseshoe shaped ring around the fire, fingers warmed by china tea cups and the hot brew within.

"Right," said Lady Weston. "Progress report?"

The Countess of Portland snatched eagerly at a biscuit and dunked it in her tea, her eyes bright with excitement. "Well, I think my work is done! Lord Trent Ballantine and a marriage proposal . . . oh, it has been a splendid evening, a splendid evening indeed for my Winnie."

Lady Weston nodded sagely. "Splendid indeed, Pamela, and ever so romantic! And you, Clare? How did your Prudence fare?"

"The girl is altogether too worried about 'being sensible' but I'm praying that she'll relax her 'sensibilities' long enough to let herself be swept off her feet by Christopher Chance."

"Perfect!" said Lady Weston, with a little clap of her hands. "And you, Lenore? What do you have to report?"

"I am happy to say that my Lettie has completely forgotten about the looming spectacle of Homer Trout in light of the fact that the Earl of Weybourne is here."

"As you had hoped he would be."

"As I was all but guaranteed by his sister that he

would be." Lenore cast a sly smile at Lady Weston. "Thanks to your Stephen, who asked him to come and evaluate a mare. It seems that the handsome young earl is no more immune to the lure of a good horse than my daughter is." She sipped her tea, grinning. "Let's just hope that neither are immune to each other."

9

Letitia opened her eyes early the next morning after a night of troubled, restless sleep. Nightmares of Simon and Lord Weybourne dueling at dawn ... reliving the sparkling joy of sitting next to the earl at the dinner table and feeling all hot and shivery inside when he'd called her beautiful ... dreams of his intense gray eyes, his warm hands, and the way his mouth had felt against her own, the way it had tasted, the way she yearned to have him kiss her again, over and over again.

He was here.

Here.

And she had another full day to get to know him.

But did he want to get to know her? After her shocking, scandalous masquerade as a boy, her deceit, and her oh-so-wanton response to his stolen kiss? Was the interest he'd paid to her last night at the table because he fancied her, or was he just being polite? What must he think of her? And what on earth had transpired between him and Simon in the *discussion* both had planned to have with the other over her?

And then she remembered Homer Trout—who was supposed to arrive today.

Her stomach somersaulted. Just when she'd found someone genuinely interesting, fascinating, and able to twist her tongue and insides into knots that would make any of the mariner men of her family proud, someone whose kiss had become something to relive over and over again in her mind, someone whose presence here was something akin to Providence ... Homer Trout was going to come here and ruin it all?

She had to do something.

Quickly.

She pushed back the covers, parted the bed hangings, and shivering, looked toward the window, only to see snow falling softly beyond the ancient panes of glass. She gasped in surprise, her worry over the looming arrival of Homer Trout forgotten. Snow! And for Christmas! Oh, how delightful!

Still in her night clothes, the hem of the garment floating around her ankles, she ran to the window seat and looked out. An inch, maybe two, had fallen overnight and it was still coming down in fat, fluffy flakes that swirled past her window and drifted down to the lawn below, now white beneath the light cover.

She rang for Beryl, begging her to hurry as the maid hastily brushed her glossy golden-brown tresses into a loose chignon, pinned it atop her head, and sent her downstairs garbed in a smart, fitted riding habit of dark blue wool that showed off the gentle rise of her breasts, her tiny waist and the flare of her hips.

The house was not yet awake. Servants were about, quietly stoking fires, laying out newspapers, and by the smell of food coming from the kitchens, preparing a breakfast grand enough to feed an army.

And still, beyond every window she passed, snow falling, drifting down from the heavy gray skies, reminding her of the fact that it was Christmastime ... and she was, by the looks of it, the only one of the guests up early enough to see and enjoy it.

She had the morning, the magic, and all of that outside beauty entirely to herself.

And here she was—inside.

Delicious smells from the kitchen and dining room beckoned her, but breakfast could wait.

She was just heading for the door when the statue that had been leaning carelessly against a recessed window in the great hall moved.

Letitia let out a little gasp of surprise, then relaxed when she realized that it was no statue, but Lord

Weybourne, who had been watching the snow falling outside.

And her.

She found her tongue. "Lord Weybourne!"

"Good morning, Miss Ponsonby. Sleep well?"

Her eyes, sparkling with amusement, met his. "Is it that obvious that I did not?"

"That's no question to be asking a gentleman who wishes to be nothing but gallant."

"Gallant? You're supposed to be helping me create a scandal so I can deter an unwanted suitor. Who cares about gallant?"

"Well, I do. But since you ask, Miss Ponsonby, you look as fresh as the snow falling from out of the sky."

"I barely slept a wink."

"And why is that?"

Because all I could think of, was you. All I could dream of was you. You, you, you.

"Because my mama was acting quite suspiciously last night. I think she knows I slipped out and visited your stable back in Norfolk. I could tell just by the way she was looking at you, the pointed intent to her questions, that she's suspicious about how and why we already know each other. Oh, she's far sharper than she lets on. If she finds out that I was at your estate, in your barn, it will be far more than a 'little scandal' I'll be getting, and you'll be dragged into it right along with me."

"I see."

"Does that not worry you?"

"Not at all." He folded his arms across his chest and smiled. "I had a nice little *discussion* with your brother last night. I asked him if he would approve of my courting you. Of course, your father is the one from whom I need official permission, but I felt I owed your brother the respect he deserves as your sibling. He was ready to call me out at dawn this morning and I wanted to settle his conscience that my intentions were honorable."

"You wish to court me?"

"If you are agreeable to the idea, of course."

It was hard to speak past the sudden dryness of her throat. "Of course," she said, hoping she didn't sound like too much of a ninny. But oh, it was hard to form words when her tongue suddenly forgot how to move, the pit of her belly was filled with butterflies, and her skin had gone all hot and prickly. "And what did my brother say?"

"He gave his consent. And what do *you* say, Miss Ponsonby?"

Say? What could she say? She could barely speak. "I would be most receptive of your attention, Lord Weybourne."

"Tristan."

"Tristan."

"And may I call you Letitia?"

She felt as though someone had poured melted butter into her very veins. "You may ... or Lettie. Or even—" her eyes sparkled with sudden humor—"Ledyard."

A door slammed somewhere upstairs and Letitia lowered her voice. "I can't be here alone with you. You know that. I know that. I must go."

"So go find a chaperone and come riding with me."

"Right now?"

"Yes, now." He reached out and took her hand, stroking the back of it once, twice, through her glove before releasing it. His very touch caused her to shiver in delight. "I've a mind to clear my head after the excesses and overindulgences of last night. Besides, you promised you would join me. What do you say, Lettie, to a good, bracing canter across the heath?"

"I would say that I'd far prefer that to staying here and finding ways to avoid Homer Trout, whose arrival is surely imminent."

"Go find a chaperone. The older, the blinder, the better."

A chaperone? At this hour? And in this weather?

Ohhhh, drat! Here she was, with the chance to ride out with Tristan St. Aubyn, to race him across a frozen heath and hope he hadn't brought one of his famed Norfolk Thoroughbreds. Or to maybe hope that he had. What to do? Her maid could not sit a horse. She knew none of the staff.

Simon. Should she ask him?

He certainly wasn't "blind" as Lord Weybourne wanted.

Footsteps were coming down the hall, and any

moment now their owner would come around the corner and catch the two of them together.

"I'll be out in the stables," Lord Weybourne murmured, and reaching up, traced the side of her jaw with a forefinger. "Don't keep me waiting. Unless I miss my guess, the snow will be stopping soon."

And with that, he gave her a little bow and was out the door in a soft whoosh of cold air and blown-in snow.

Letitia reached up and cupped the side of her jaw with her palm, trying to hold in his touch. Oh, what to do? Her blood began to thrum. *Chaperone ... chaperone....*

She hurried back toward the dining room.

Simon was up, sitting alone at the long table. He was leaning back in a chair, a newspaper at his elbow and a cup of black coffee before him. His back was toward her; he had not seen her. He was dressed in civilian clothes, a dark gray coat with a high-standing collar cut to fit his fine form perfectly, his hair thick and handsome and resisting the brush's attempts to coax it into a neat, orderly fashion. He looked helplessly windblown, even when he wasn't standing on the quarterdeck of his frigate, and Letitia figured that made him pretty much irresistible to the ladies.

His expression this morning though was brooding.

Chaperone?

No. Not Simon. Her brother might have consented to Lord Weybourne's courtship of her, but he was too upstanding, too protective, to let the two of them out of his sight if he was called upon to accompany them.

The devil take a chaperone. She had no time to find one anyhow, and she suddenly knew what she must do.

If she got caught, the whole house party would come crashing down around her ears. But she was young. She was clever.

And nobody was up yet anyhow.

10

Tristan had just selected two hunters—one bay, the other a strapping chestnut—from the Weston stables and was helping the sleepy groom tack them up when Letitia came silently in from outside, snow frosting her little round hat and the cold pulling roses from her cheeks. Her eyes were bright with excitement.

He quickly moved away from the groom, his brows rising in surprise. "No chaperone?"

"The house is asleep. We'll take our gallop across the heath and be back before anyone is even stirring." She glanced over her shoulder through the falling snow to the quiet majesty of the mansion behind them, but no outraged brother, mother or anyone else was charging through the falling snow to stop her. "That is, if you're game."

"If your mama or anyone else finds out, it'll be more

than just a 'little scandal' you'll find yourself dealing with."

"I am good at this. Very good." She grinned and moved further into the stable, her feminine curves shown to perfection by a close-fitting riding habit that made him want to devour her with his eyes. His hands. His mouth. "Did you bring one of your Norfolk Thoroughbreds?"

"I did not. The herd isn't built up enough yet to be using one as my own personal mount."

"Perhaps it will be a fair race, then. Let's be off before the snow stops."

"Are you certain you want to risk this?"

"We'll head out the back of the stables and into the fields. They can't see that from the house, even if someone does happen to wake and look out the window. It will be worth the risk."

Yes, it will be, he thought. He liked her brazen confidence. It was infectious, seductive, and it made him want to take her into his arms and kiss her until she couldn't see straight. No simpering little miss was the Honourable Miss Letitia Ponsonby; she was like a breath of fresh air through a hot, stale room. Or maybe, he thought wryly, more like a hurricane wind.

The groom had led the two horses out into the aisle. The chestnut stood pawing the stone floor, his hooves echoing in the close confines.

"This is going to be fun," she said, her eyes glowing.

She lifted the flap of the saddle to check the girth, pulled the billets up another hole, and let the flap settle back down. "Are you ready, Lord Weybourne?"

Oh, the girl had spirit, he'd give her that. And a reckless bravery that was going to land them both in plenty of hot water if any of this got out. He looked at her standing there, a vision in blue, so deliciously beautiful that the sight of her left his mouth dry and his tongue all but cleaved to the roof of his mouth. But oh, it wasn't just her beauty that had his blood warming his veins on this cold and snowy morning. It was her boldness, her courage, her complete confidence that all would turn out exactly as she wanted it to.

"So you need a little scandal to put off this Homer person," he mused. "Do you think your father will deny my intentions and favor this Homer Trout person's suit instead?"

"I don't know, but Mama did invite him here, so she obviously has plans. If I can create just a bit of scandal, perhaps he'll decide that I'm too wild, too controversial, to take an interest in, and that will put a swift end to his intensions—and Mama's plans."

"What kind of scandal are you considering, Letitia?"

"I don't know yet. It was a matter of deep discussion last night with my friends Pru, Winnie and Jane, and none of us came up with anything that might possibly work." She led her horse to a nearby mounting block. "I'm told the men will be going shooting this afternoon but perhaps at dinner tonight, you can help me create a minor disturbance." She paused, catching her lower lip between her teeth, worrying it in a way that caused it to swell and redden prettily and the breath to catch in Tristan's lungs. "Perhaps —" she yanked down a stirrup iron and turned to look at him— "perhaps I will spill some of my drink on myself and you will grab a napkin and try to wipe it off in front of everyone, and I will pretend I'm outraged and Mr. Trout will question not only my grace and elegance, but your touching me so boldly—"

He laughed. "Should I take such a liberty, it won't be Mr. Trout who will be questioning you, it will be your brother questioning *me*, and demanding to meet me at dawn with pistols or swords."

She made a little dismissive gesture with her hand. "That is absurd."

"Is it? He is your brother. A very by-the-book, overprotective brother, unless I miss my guess. He will be bound to defend your honor. Not that I'm afraid of meeting him or anyone else at dawn, but if we end up killing each other it would be dreadfully unfair to both you and your family."

"You worry too much, Lord Weybourne."

"Lettie, I did not come down here to look for a wife," he said, trying to sound convincing.

"And I did not come down here to look for a husband."

"I have no time for a wife. My horses and my estate

keep me busy. I only came here to determine the quality of a mare that Stephen Pemberly asked me to evaluate."

"And I have no time for a husband. I only came here because I had no choice."

"You could have joined my employ and stayed at my estate in Norfolk."

"I could have, as insane and impossible as the idea is. But you kissed me and ruined everything. I had to leave after that."

"You didn't *have* to."

They stood looking at each other, each thinking of that stolen kiss and yearning for a way to repeat it.

Letitia allowed him to hold her mare while she climbed the mounting block, stepped into the stirrup iron, and mounted the horse. She looked down at him, smiling and wishing she dared to reach out and wipe away the snowflakes melting on his cheeks. "We should leave before the house begins to wake."

"We should. Because if we stand here gazing at each other for any longer, I might give into temptation, and then we will most surely be delayed."

"What temptation?"

"The temptation to pull you down from that saddle, take you into my arms and kiss you."

"Oh!" She flushed pink and hot, but her eyes sparkled and for once, she was at a loss for words.

"Oh!" he mimicked playfully, his own eyes warming in

a way that made her heart skip a beat and then two. He took her gloved hand in his own and drew it down to his lips, letting them linger for a long moment on the back of her fingers. "So where do we go from here?"

She gazed down at her knuckles against his lips, smiling foolishly. "How about for our ride, to start?"

"A perfect idea," he said, reluctantly relinquishing her hand. Still flustered, she gathered up her reins and watched as he swung up onto his own mount. Together they trotted away from the back of the stables and across the frozen pasture, where the snow had already obliterated the grass and left everything mantled in white.

"WHY LENORE, WHATEVER DO YOU FIND SO fascinating outside that window?"

The four mamas were breakfasting on tea and rolls in a small drawing room, but Viscountess Penmore, sipping thoughtfully from her teacup, was standing by the great windows and looking outside into the snow.

Except she wasn't looking outside into the snow, but down through the snow and toward the stables below where, in the gloom of an open door, she could see two well-bred hunters standing saddled and ready for a ride.

"Lord Weybourne," she said, taking another sip from her cup. "And my daughter."

The other women, with Lady Weston in the lead, hustled over to join her at the window.

"I don't see Letitia anywhere," said Lady Portland.

"If you stand here long enough, you'll see her pass before the open door of the stable," said Lenore with satisfaction. "Along with Lord Weybourne. Those are their footprints in the snow, leading into the stables."

The others pressed to the window. Lady Carlisle gasped in shock. "My goodness! You are correct!"

"Do note that she is with a man," Lenore said, taking another sip. "Without a chaperone."

"This is *quite* beyond the pale!"

"Yes, delightfully so." The viscountess looked like a cat that had just finished off a bowl of cream. "The perfect scandal, I should think."

Lady Weston put her hand to her open mouth, her eyes dancing beneath her pretense of horrified shock. "Someone will have to discover them, of course."

"Trust me, Someone will." She tapped a finger against her top lip. "Time to get my darling Simon roused, enraged, and engaged in his brotherly duty, I think. He has a sister whose honor must be defended."

"Oh, do hurry, Lenore. In case your Letitia comes to her senses before you can get her neatly trapped."

The viscountess grinned, excitement making her look more like a youthful maiden than a conniving mama. "My daughter abandoned her senses the moment she met the dashing and devastatingly handsome Lord Weybourne.

And by the look of him last night, the feeling is mutual."
She drained her tea, set the empty cup and saucer down
on the silver tray on the table, and headed for the door.
Now, if you will excuse me, ladies? I have a daughter to
marry off."

☙ 11 ☙

It was slippery on the cobblestones, slippery on the short, clipped grass of the lawn, but once out in the pastures where the footing was rougher and more secure, they gave the horses, fretting, prancing, and impatient to be off, their heads.

"Race you!" Letitia cried, leaning forward and pressing her heels and calves to her mount's side. The big bay mare all but burst out from beneath her, and laughing, Letitia let her go, the falling snowflakes stinging her face, frosting her eyelashes, the cold wind whipping her cheeks. Beneath her, the steady, rapid thunder of the horse's hooves was a familiar thrill. She glanced to her right and saw Tristan keeping pace. He was a natural rider, Letitia thought in admiration, his hands giving and taking in time to the lunge and pull-back of the horse's head with each stride, his seat secure, relaxed and effortless.

Ahead was a copse of pine, dark against the gray sky. They slowed their mounts to a walk to let them cool down, plumes of steam blowing from the horses' wide and flaring nostrils, the snow still whispering down all around them.

"That was fun," Letitia said breathlessly.

"You are a fine rider, Lettie."

"You aren't so bad yourself."

She grinned, her eyes sparkling, quietly wishing him closer. He seemed to have the same idea for a moment later he'd urged his horse nearer to her own so that his thigh was nearly touching her skirts. *Shocking,* she thought. *Delightful.*

"Do you know what I would love to do someday?" she asked, her heartbeat picking up at his nearness and a breathless sense of need, of longing, heating her blood.

"What is that?"

"When he is old enough, I would love to help you train Amir to saddle. To gain his trust, to be the first one on his back, to feel him fly like Pegasus beneath me."

His smile warmed. "There are very few people to whom I would entrust such a task, but you, Lettie, would be the first person I would ask."

Her eyes grew dreamy. "Are they really that fast?" she asked. "These horses that your father developed?"

"They are really that fast." They had reached the copse and the snow whispered silently down around them, mysterious, beautiful, lovely. Already, the sweeping boughs of pine were mantled with white, bowing beneath the weight. Tristan halted his horse and dismounted, holding the reins of both animals while helping Letitia to do the same. She landed lightly on her feet. "And there is no greater thrill on earth than to ride one, except, maybe this."

"This?"

He moved closer, so close that she could feel the heat emanating from his body as he transferred the reins to one hand and slid the other beneath the tails of her riding habit, his fingers warm against her hips, now finding that perfect little spot in the hollow of her back with which to draw her close. "This."

And with that, he bent his head and kissed her.

Letitia melted beneath the onslaught of his lips like the snow that whispered down around them. She was aware of nothing but him. Of the heat of his hand, pressing against the small of her back and drawing her closer to him. Of the hard length of his body, of the feel of his powerful arms. Of his mouth, closing over hers with firm insistence, impatient and demanding, slanting now as his tongue came out and licked at the seam of her lips. She hesitantly opened to him and he plunged inside, the sudden shock of his tongue against hers, in her mouth, sending a jolt of pleasure radiating through her blood and out into the nipples of her breasts. He tasted of the orange he must have had for breakfast, tart and delicious, of sharp cold air, melted snow and hot passion. She felt his fingers stroking the curve of her bottom, tracing it, pulling her even closer up against him. She made a little sigh of contentment deep in her throat, and reaching up, finally did what she'd been longing to do yet again, sliding her hands up into his hair, wet now with melted snow, relishing the silken softness of it, the loose, short, glossy waves and curls threading through her fingers as she molded her hands to the sides of his skull. Standing on tiptoe, she pushed herself more urgently against his mouth and into his embrace.

Snow fell from the sky, tingling and melting against her face, against his. A now-familiar ache began somewhere in the pit of her belly, in the junction of her thighs, and she knew it for what it was:

Desire.

He felt it, too. His mouth slanted against hers, growing more insistent, more persistent, and Letitia moaned as the ache between her legs strengthened and became almost piercing.

He broke the kiss for the shortest of moments to loop the reins of the horses over a low branch, then they were together once more, both growing desperate, his hands driving between the closure of her riding jacket, pushing beneath the heavy wool to shape her waist, her hips, her bottom. Fiercely, he pulled her pelvis up against him, his cupped hands roving lower and down toward the back of her thighs, lower still, until she felt his fingers gently stroking her down *there*.

Letitia let out a little gasp and pulled away, dropping her hot forehead against his open coat.

"Kiss me like you mean it," he murmured, his voice husky.

"I don't know how," she said in a little voice. "It's not like I've done this before."

"Then let me show you." Again, his mouth lowered to hers, and he angled his head so their noses wouldn't touch, so that their mouths fitted perfectly together, so that he could grind his mouth against hers and force his own tongue against her own, until she was kissing him back with a passion that left her breathless and dizzy.

Snow tingled cold and wet upon her forehead, her nose. She made a little sound of joy deep in her throat and pulling back, rested her forehead against his chest once more, trying to catch her breath. He was breathing as hard as she, and she heard and felt his heart beating frantically beneath his coat. She looked up at him, and he took her face within his hands, gently thumbing her cheekbones as he gazed down into her eyes.

"I've been wanting to do that since you ran away back in Norfolk," he said hoarsely.

"And I've been regretting that I ran away."

"No more regrets for either of us, Lettie." His gray eyes darkened, crinkling a bit at the corners as he smiled down at her and gently stroked her cheek. "Just gratitude. You're here. I'm here, and I'm glad of it. Glad that I put down my work, my endless pursuit of rebuilding my fortune in order to relax. To come look at a horse that I still haven't seen."

"Maybe there isn't one," she said, thinking of how much manipulation had already taken place, and not finding it in her heart to resent any of it.

"Maybe there isn't. And I don't care." He lowered his lips and let them brush her forehead, warming it against the melting snow. "I almost didn't come, you know. Figured I didn't have time, couldn't take or make the time to get away."

"But it's Christmas, Tristan."

"It's Christmas."

"Stand here with me and feel the peace and joy of the season," she murmured, snuggling up against him and feeling his arms tighten around her, his cheek resting against the top of her head until she felt perfectly enclosed within his presence. At home. And in a place where she knew she'd belonged since time began. "Feel it all around us ... in the silence, in the stillness, in the beauty of this deep, quiet world as the snow drifts down around us. Life is not all work and the pursuit of goals, Tristan. Once in a while, we all have to stop to smell the roses ... to note the beauty of this world that God created for us ... to stand in a cold stable and gaze with wonder and joy at the child in the manger." She bent back and looked up in to his eyes. "Happy Christmas, Tristan."

"Happy Christmas, Lettie."

He smiled, bent his head to kiss her once more and at that moment, one of the horses flung up its head and let out a long, piercing whinny, startling them both.

In the split second that it took for Tristan to set her back and firmly away from him, Letitia saw another horse some fifty feet away. Saw the dark blue sea coat, the cocked hat, the anger and murderous fury in her brother's piercing stare.

Her heart dropped from her throat into her knees.

"S-Simon," she said weakly.

But he had dismounted and was walking toward them.

He had seen everything. It was too late.

Simon's voice could have carried the length of a quarterdeck.

"Letitia!"

He didn't quite roar, but he didn't have to; Simon was a commanding enough figure, a man whose authority was ingrained, recognizable, unmistakable to anyone within or beyond his sphere. Letitia flushed crimson and hastily stepped back, her mind whirling from Tristan's kiss, the shock of being discovered, the necessity of finding a way out of this rapidly deteriorating situation.

"Good morning, Captain Ponsonby," said Tristan affably. "I know what this looks like and I can assure you that it is—"

"I know what the situation looks like!" This time, Simon actually *did* roar.

"—as I was about to say, I can assure you that it is *exactly* what it looks like it is." Tristan was composed, confident, and if looks were to be believed, not one iota upset or embarrassed by the situation in which Simon had caught them. "I was kissing your sister. I enjoyed kissing your sister, and I would enjoy getting to know her as my *wife* even better, if you will give your informal consent, Captain, and your father, his official one."

Not much took Simon aback, but such a declaration was not what he was expecting. Sheepish excuses, yes. Stammered apologies, perhaps. Even an acceptance of the challenge to meet him at dawn that would have been his next demand. But marriage?

"Captain?" prompted Lord Weybourne.

"You barely know her," Simon muttered, looking from one to the other.

"I know her well enough that I'm certain I would like to spend the rest of my life with her. Isn't that enough?"

Letitia had been silently watching this tense exchange. Now, she raised her chin and sidled closer to

Tristan, her heart topsy-turvy, her senses reeling at the speed with which things were happening.

Marriage?

"What about you, Lettie?" her brother asked. "Have you nothing to say, for once in your life?"

She colored and kicked at the snow with the toe of her boot. "Well ... I rather enjoyed being kissed by Lord Weybourne. And I would be honored to be his wife."

"This is the most half-baked proposal—and acceptance—I've ever heard." Simon narrowed his eyes, frowning. "That's it? You two both think you'll suit because you enjoy each other's kisses?"

"We both like horses, Letitia said stubbornly. "And he has kept my secret safe. I trust him."

"What secret?"

"I sneaked out to his estate while we were visiting Lady Ariadne in Norfolk, on the way here. I only wanted to see his horses ... and try to figure a way out of this dreadful house party in which I'm to be married off to the abominable Mr. Homer Trout."

"What?"

"Homer Trout. Don't be obtuse, Simon. The skinny, insipid man with the mole on his nose and the bristle growing out of it."

Her brother shook his head in confusion and impatience. "What nonsense are you talking about?"

"Did you not know? I overheard Mama talking to Lady Adriane. She was telling her that Mr. Trout would be at this house party and that her intention was to see me married to him as I've been on the marriage market for three Seasons now, and Mama was despairing of me ever finding a match. She'd had enough." Tristan extended his hand to her and she took it, grateful for the reassuring squeeze of his fingers around her own. "I do not want to marry Homer Trout, Simon. I never did. I ran off that afternoon in the hopes I could clear my head enough that I could think of a way out of Mama's plans for me. And maybe even this party."

"Homer Trout is not at this party. I don't know what you're talking about."

"He is supposed to arrive today. Tristan and I were going to create a ... a little scandal so that Homer would think me too wild and unsuitable and no longer be interested in me."

"For one thing," Simon said, raising a hand and ticking off his points on his fingers, "Homer Trout is not at this party," he repeated firmly. "And he is not going to be. He was never invited and he is already married."

"What?"

"Mama only told you that so you'd do exactly what you've gone and done. Get yourself into trouble such that you'd have to get married to someone far more suitable. Someone of your own choosing."

Letitia's mouth opened in a silent "O" and beside her, Tristan's lips began to twitch.

"Secondly," Simon continued, "you have indeed

created a scandal. Mama and her busy-body friends all saw you in the stable with Lord Weybourne, and knew you'd gone out riding with him alone. Mama came and got me and told me to retrieve you." As Letitia went white, he added, a bit more gently, "Everyone knows, Letitia."

"Everyone?"

"Everyone."

"Oh," she said in a little voice, and pressed her fingers to her mouth.

"Thirdly," he said darkly, "I have learned from Stephen that this little house party was never solely about a bunch of friends and acquaintances celebrating the Yuletide and making merry. It was about marrying off four daughters who have evaded husbands on the marriage mart for the past two or three Seasons. Lord Trent Ballantine has offered for Lady Winifred Grisham. Chalk one up to the four mamas. Now, Lord Weybourne here has offered for you, Letitia. Chalk two up to the four mamas. That leaves just Lady Prudence and Lady Jane, and I would bet every gun on my frigate and the powder to fire them that the four mamas will have their betrothals done and dusted before Boxing Day arrives and we all start making plans to leave."

Letitia walked a little distance away and leaned against the bay mare's side. Her head was swimming. Mama, plotting her marriage? The other ladies doing the same with their daughters, her friends?

"This is all rather amusing," Tristan said at last. "Why is it when you put several females together, the world gets turned on its ear?"

"Because that's the way females are," Simon said, as though that fact was obvious. "Not happy unless they're meddling, manipulating, and marrying people off. My God, I wouldn't be a bit surprised if they have plans for me, too. Glad I'm going back to sea. I'd rather take my chances with the French." He looked squarely at Tristan and then at Letitia. "So now that you both know you've been neatly manipulated by Mama and perhaps, Weybourne, even your sister, do you still want to go through with this marriage, or do we have a date at dawn with either pistols or swords?"

"Manipulated or not, it does not change my offer, or my interest in your sister," Tristan said firmly.

"And you, Letitia?"

"Well, I admit that it rather stings that Mama felt pressed to take matters into her own hands, but it does not change my interest in Lord Weybourne's suit."

Simon's taciturn features relaxed in a reluctant smile. "Well, then," he said at last, "at least you both have plenty in common. Are you as horse-mad as my sister is, Weybourne?"

"Do ships float?"

"Only until they go aground or get shot to pieces and sunk."

Tristan, smiling, drew Letitia close. "This ship that

will be our marriage will not, to use your analogy, go aground or get shot to pieces. I pledge to you, Captain Ponsonby, that I will love and treasure your sister for all the days of my life."

"Letitia?"

"For once, I am grateful to Mama for interfering. If she hadn't waved the spectacle of Homer Trout behind a temptingly closed door, I might never have gone to Tristan's estate in the hopes of delaying this trip." She smiled up at Tristan. "If I've spent every waking moment, and most of my dreaming ones, thinking of you, does that mean that I'm in love?"

He laughed and pulled her close, uncaring that her brother was standing nearby. "It means that you and I share a similar affliction, because I have found myself unable to think of anyone or anything but you since you sneaked into my stable and won over Amir's heart ... and in that moment, I daresay, mine as well."

Around them, the snow whispered down, frosting their hair, melting on their cheeks.

Peace. Joy. Stillness. And the greatest gift of the Christmas season.

Love.

"Turn your back, Captain Ponsonby," said Tristan, pulling his fiancée into his arms and gazing down at her with his heart in his eyes. "We are about to seal our promise with a kiss."

Above them, the bough of a pine drooped under the growing weight of the snow.

It wasn't quite mistletoe, but as Tristan lowered his head and let his lips claim Letitia's, both of them knew that it would do quite nicely.

That it was, in fact, Perfect.

A HEARTFELT THANK YOU!

Thank you from the bottom of my heart for reading my book. If you enjoyed it, please consider posting a review. Reviews don't just help the author, they help other readers discover our books and, no matter how long or short, I sincerely appreciate every review.

Would you like to know when my next book is available? Sign up for my newsletter:

Also, please follow me on BookBub to be notified of deals and new releases.

Thank you again for reading and for your support.

PREVIEW THE WILD ONE

BOOK 1 OF THE DE MONTFORTE BROTHERS SERIES

BY DANELLE HARMON

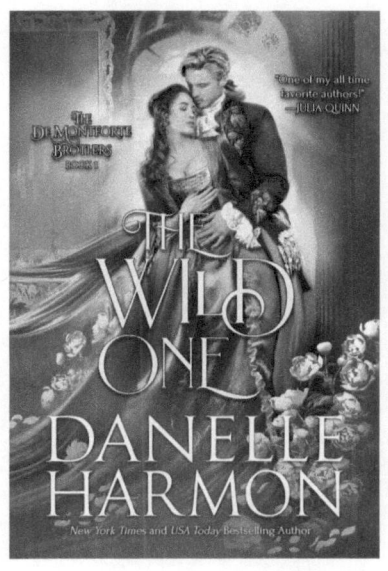

Get your copy of The Wild One today!

PROLOGUE

Newman House, 18 April, 1775

My dear brother, Lucien,

It has just gone dark and as I pen these words to you, an air of rising tension hangs above this troubled town. Tonight, several regiments — including mine, the King's Own — have been ordered by General Gage, commander in chief of our forces here in Boston, out to Concord to seize and destroy a significant store of arms and munitions that the rebels have secreted there. Due to the clandestine nature of this assignment, I have ordered my batman, Billingshurst, to withhold the posting of this letter until the morrow, when the mission will have been completed and secrecy will no longer be of concern.

Although it is my most ardent hope that no blood will be shed on either side during this endeavour, I find that my heart, in these final moments before I must leave, is restless and uneasy. It is not for myself that I am afraid, but another. As you know from my previous letters home, I have met a young woman here with whom I have become attached in a warm friendship. I suspect you do not approve of my becoming so enamoured of a storekeeper's daughter, but things are different in this place, and when a fellow is three thousand miles away from home, love makes a far more desirable companion than loneliness. My dear Miss Paige has made me happy, Lucien, and earlier tonight, she accepted my plea for her hand in marriage; I beg you to understand, and forgive, for I know that someday when you meet her, you will love her as I do.

My brother, I have but one thing to ask of you, and knowing that you will see to my wishes is the only thing that calms my troubled soul during these last few moments before we depart. If anything should happen to me — tonight, tomorrow, or at any time whilst I am here in Boston — I beg of you to find it in your heart to show charity and kindness to my angel, my Juliet, for she means the world to me. I know you will take care of her if ever I cannot. Do this for me and I shall be happy, Lucien.

I must close now, as the others are gathered downstairs in the parlour, and we are all ready to move. May God bless and keep you, my dear brother, and Gareth, Andrew, and sweet Nerissa, too.

Charles

S ometime during the last hour, it had begun to grow dark.

Lucien de Montforte turned the letter over in his hands, his gaze shuttered, his mind far away as he stared out the window over the downs that stood like sentinels against the fading twilight. A breath of pink still glowed in the western sky, but it would soon be gone. He hated this time of night, this still and lonely hour just after sunset when old ghosts were near, and distant memories welled up in the heart with the poignant nearness of yesterday, close enough to see yet always too elusive to touch.

But the letter was real. Too real.

He ran a thumb over the heavy vellum, the bold, elegant script that had been so distinctive of Charles's style — both on paper, in thought, and on the field — still looking as fresh as if it had been written yesterday, not last April. His own name was there on the front: *To His Grace the Duke of Blackheath, Blackheath Castle, nr. Ravenscombe, Berkshire, England.*

They were probably the last words Charles had ever written.

Carefully, he folded the letter along creases that had become fragile and well-worn. The blob of red wax with which his brother had sealed the letter came together at the edges like a wound that had never healed, and try as he might to avoid seeing them, his gaze caught the words that someone, probably Billingshurst, had written on the back....

Found on the desk of Captain Lord Charles Adair de Montforte on the 19th of April 1775, the day on which his lordship was killed in the fighting at Concord. Please deliver to addressee.

A pang went through him. Dead, gone, and all but forgotten, just like that.

The Duke of Blackheath carefully laid the letter inside the drawer, which he shut and locked. He gazed once more out the window, lord of all he surveyed but unable to master his own bitter emptiness. A mile away, at the foot of the downs, he could just see the twinkling lights of Ravenscombe village, could envision its ancient church with its Norman tower and tombs of de Montforte dead. And there, inside, high on the stone wall of the chancel, was the simple bronze plaque that was all they had to tell posterity that his brother had ever even lived.

Charles, the second son.

God help them all if anything happened to him, Lucien, and the dukedom passed to the third.

No. God would not be so cruel.

He snuffed the single candle and with the darkness enclosing him, the sky still glowing beyond the window, moved from the room.

BERKSHIRE, ENGLAND, 1776

The Flying White was bound for Oxford, and it was running late. Now, trying to make up time lost to a broken axle, the driver had whipped up the team, and the coach careered through the night in a cacophony of shouts, thundering hooves, and cries from the passengers who were clinging for their lives on the roof above.

Strong lanterns cut through the rainy darkness, picking out ditches, trees, and hedgerows as the vehicle hurtled through the Lambourn Downs at a pace that had Juliet Paige's heart in her throat. Because of Char-lotte, her six-month-old daughter, Juliet had been lucky enough to get a seat inside the coach, but even so, her head banged against the leather squabs on the right, her shoulder against an elderly gent on her left, and her neck ached with the constant side to side movement. On the seat across from her, another young mother clung to her two frightened children, one huddled under each arm. It had been a dreadful run up from Southampton indeed, and Juliet was feeling almost as ill as she had during the long sea voyage over from Boston.

The coach hit a bump, became airborne for a split second, and landed hard, snapping her neck, throwing her violently against the man on her left, and causing the passengers clinging to the roof above to cry out in terror. Someone's trunk went flying off the coach, but the driver never slowed the galloping team.

"God help us!" murmured the young mother across from Juliet as her children cringed fearfully against her.

Juliet grasped the strap and hung her head, fighting nausea as she hugged her own child. Her lips touched the baby's downy gold curls. "Almost there," she whispered, for Charlotte's ears alone. "Almost there—to your papa's home."

Suddenly without warning, there were shouts, a horse's frightened whinny, and violent curses from the driver. Someone on the roof screamed. The coach careened madly, the inhabitants both inside and out shrieking in terror as the vehicle hurtled along on two wheels for another forty or fifty feet before finally crashing heavily down on its axles with another neck-snapping jolt, shattering a window with the impact and spilling the elderly gent to the floor. Outside, someone was sobbing in fear and pain.

And inside, the atmosphere of the coach went as still as death.

"We're being robbed!" cried the old man, getting to his knees to peer out the rain-spattered window.

Shots rang out. There was a heavy thud from above, then movement just beyond the ominous black pane. And then suddenly, without warning it imploded, showering the inside passengers in a hail of glass.

Gasping, they looked up to see a heavy pistol—and a masked face just beyond it.

"Yer money or yer life. *Now!*"

IT WAS THE VERY DEVIL OF A NIGHT. NO MOON, NO stars, and a light rain stinging his face as Lord Gareth Francis de Montforte sent his horse, Crusader, flying down the Wantage road at a speed approaching suicide. Stands of beech and oak shot past, there then gone. Pounding hooves splashed through puddles and echoed against the hedgerows that bracketed the road. Gareth glanced over his shoulder, saw nothing but a long empty stretch of road behind him, and shouted with glee. Another race won—Perry, Chilcot, and the rest of the Den of Debauchery would never catch him now!

Laughing, he patted Crusader's neck as the hunter pounded through the night. "Well done, good fellow! Well done—"

And pulled him up sharply at he passed Wether Down.

It took him only a moment to assess the situation.

Highwaymen. And by the looks of it, they were helping themselves to the pickings—and passengers—of the Flying White from Southampton.

The Flying White? The young gentleman reached inside his coat pocket and pulled out his watch, squinting to see its face in the darkness. Damned late for the Flying White . . .

He dropped the timepiece back into his pocket, steadied Crusader, and considered what to do. No gentlemen of the road, this lot, but a trio of desperate, hardened killers. The driver and guard lay on the ground beside the coach, both presumably dead. Somewhere a child was crying, and now one of the bandits, with a face that made a hatchet look kind, smashed in the windows of the coach with the butt end of his gun. Gareth reached for his pistol. The thought of quietly turning around and going back the way he'd come never occurred to him. The thought of waiting for his friends, probably a mile behind thanks to Crusader's blistering speed, didn't occur to him, either. Especially when he saw one of the bandits yank open the door of the coach and haul out a struggling young woman.

He had just the briefest glimpse of her face—scared, pale, beautiful—before one of the highwaymen shot out the lanterns of the coach and darkness fell over the entire scene. Someone screamed. Another shot rang out, silencing the frightened cry abruptly.

His face grim, the young gentleman knotted his horse's reins and removed his gloves, pulling each one carefully off by the fingertips. With a watchful eye on the highwaymen, he slipped his feet from the irons and vaulted lightly down from the thoroughbred's tall back, his glossy top boots of Spanish leather landing in chalk mud up to his ankles. The horse never moved. He doffed his fine new surtout and laid it over the saddle along with his tricorn and gloves. He tucked the lace at his wrist safely inside his sleeve to protect it from any soot or sparks his pistol might emit. Then he crept through the knee-high weeds and nettles that grew thick at the side of the road, priming and loading the pistol as he moved stealthily toward the stricken coach. He would have time to squeeze off only one shot before they were upon him, and that one shot had to count.

"Everybo'y out. *Now!*"

Holding Charlotte tightly against her, Juliet managed to remain calm as the robber snared her wrist and jerked her violently from the vehicle. She landed awkwardly in the sticky white mud and would have gone down if not for the huge, bearlike hand that yanked her to her feet. Perhaps, she thought numbly, it was the very fact that it *was* bearlike that she was able to keep her head—and her wits—about her, for Juliet had been born and raised in the woods of Maine, and she was no stranger to bears, Indians, and a host of other threats that made these English highwaymen look benign by comparison.

But they were certainly not benign. The slain driver lay face-down in the mud. The bodies of one of the guards and a passenger were sprawled in the weeds nearby. A shudder went through her. She was glad of the darkness. Glad that the poor little children still inside the coach were spared the horrors that daylight would have revealed.

Cuddling Charlotte, she stood beside the other passengers as the robbers yanked people down from the roof and lined them up in front of the coach. A woman was sobbing. A girl clung pitifully to the old man, perhaps her grandfather. One fellow, finely dressed and obviously a gentleman, angrily protested the treatment of the women and without a word, one of the highwayman stuck his pistol into his belly and shot him dead. As he fell, the wretched group gasped in dismay and horror. Then the last passengers were dragged from the coach, the two children clinging to their mother's skirts and crying piteously.

They all huddled together in the rainy darkness, too terrified to speak as, one by one, they were relieved of their money, their jewels, their watches, and their pride.

And then the bandits came to Juliet.

"Gimme yer money, girl, all of it. Now!"

Juliet complied. Without a sound, she handed over her reticule.

"The necklace, too."

Her hand went to her throat. Hesitated. The robber cuffed it away in impatience, ripping the thin gold chain from her neck and dropping the miniature of Charlotte's dead father into his leather bag.

"Any jewels?"

She was still staring at the bag. "No."

"Any rings?"

"No."

But he grabbed her hand, held it up, and saw it: a promise made but broken by death. It was Charles's signet ring—her engagement ring—the last thing her beloved fiancé had given her before he had died in the fighting at Concord.

"Filthy lyin' bitch, give it to me!"

Juliet stood her ground. She looked him straight in the eye and firmly, quietly, repeated the single word.

"*No.*"

Without warning he backhanded her across the cheek, and she fell to her knees in the mud, cutting her palm on a stone as she tried to prevent injury to the baby. Her hair tumbled down around her face. Charlotte began screaming. And Juliet looked up, only to see the black hole of a pistol's mouth two inches away, the robber behind it snarling with rage.

Her life passed before her eyes.

And at that moment a shot rang out from somewhere off to her right, a dark rose exploded on the highwayman's chest, and with a look of surprise, he pitched forward, dead.

ONLY ONE SHOT, BUT BY GOD, I MADE IT COUNT.

The other two highwaymen jerked around at the bark of Gareth's pistol. Their faces mirrored disbelief as they took in his fine shirt and lace at throat and sleeve, his silk waistcoat, expensive boots, expensive breeches, expensive everything. They saw him as a plum ripe for the picking, and Gareth knew it. He went for his sword.

"Get on your horses and go, and neither of you shall be hurt."

For a moment, neither the highwaymen nor the passengers moved. Then, slowly, one of the highwayman began to smile. The other, to sneer.

"Now!" Gareth commanded, still moving forward and trying to bluff them with his display of cool authority.

And then all hell broke loose.

Tongues of flame cracked from the highwaymen's pistols and Gareth heard the low whine of a ball passing at close range. Passengers screamed and dived for cover. The coach horses reared, whinnying in fear. Gareth, his sword raised, charged through the tangle of nettle that grew dense at the side of the road, trying to get to the robbers before they could reload and fire. His foot hit a patch of mud and he went down, his cheek slamming into the stinging nettles. One of the highwayman came racing toward him, spewing a torrent of foul language and intent only on finishing him off. Gareth lay gasping, then flung himself hard to the left as the bandit's pistol coughed another spear of flame. Where his shoulder had been, a plume of mud shot several inches into the air.

The brigand was still coming, roaring at the top of his lungs, already bringing up a second pistol.

Gamely, Gareth tried to get to his feet and reach his sword. He slipped in the wet weeds, his cheek on fire as though he'd been stung by a hundred bees. He was outnumbered, his pistol spent, his sword just out of reach. But he wasn't done for. Not yet. Not by any stretch of the imagination. He lunged for his sword, rolled onto his back, and sitting up, flung the weapon at the oncoming highwayman with all his strength.

The blade caught the robber just beneath the jaw and nearly took his head off. He went over backward, clawing at his throat, his dying breath a terrible, rasping gurgle.

And then Gareth saw one of the two children running toward him, obviously thinking he was the only safety left in this world gone mad.

"Billy!" the mother was screaming. "Billy, no, *get back!"*

The last highwayman spun around. Wild-eyed and desperate, he saw the fleeing child, saw that his two friends were dead, and, as though to avenge a night gone wrong, brought his pistol up, training it on the little boy's back.

"Billeeeeeeee!"

Gareth lunged to his feet, threw himself at the child, and tumbled him to the ground, shielding him with his body. The pistol exploded at close range, deafening him, a white-hot lance of fire ripping through his ribs as he rolled over and over through grass and weeds and nettles, the child still in his arms.

He came to rest upon his back, the wet weeds beneath him, blood gushing hotly from his side. He lay still, blinking up at the trees, the rain falling gently upon his throbbing cheek.

His fading mind echoed his earlier words. *Well done, good fellow! Well done . . .*

The child sprang up and ran, sobbing, back to his mother.

And for Lord Gareth de Montforte, all went dark . . .

**If you enjoyed this excerpt,
continue reading The Wild One!**

My Lady Pirate

Wicked at Heart

Lord of the Sea

Heir to the Sea

Never Too Late for Love

THE NOBLE LORDS

Master of My Dreams

Taken by Storm

Scandal at Christmas

My Saving Grace

Pirate in My Arms

ABOUT THE AUTHOR

New York Times and *USA Today* bestselling author Danelle Harmon has written many critically acclaimed and award-winning books. A Mass-achusetts native, she has lived in Great Britain, though these days she and her English  husband make their home in New England with their daughter Emma and numerous animals including three dogs, an Egyptian Arabian horse, and a flock of pet chickens. Danelle welcomes email from her readers and can be reached at Danelle@danelleharmon.com or through any of the means listed below:

CONNECT WITH ME ONLINE!
Danelle Harmon's Website
Danelle Harmon's Blog

Want to know when the next new title from Danelle is released? Click here!

Even more ways to connect: